A NOTE FROM THE AUTHOR

KT-456-437

When Dax Jones first showed up in my head, skinny, dark-eyed and restless, I had no idea how much he was going to mean to me. As a journalist I interviewed a lot of celebrities. They were fun—but the best stories I ever got were not from celebs. They came from normal people whose lives had been suddenly changed in some unexpected way. They were the *real* deal.

So Dax showed up kind of ordinary. And yet not. His name is a clue. Half ordinary, half extraordinary. I wanted to write about supernatural stuff but not in a wifty-wafty way. I wanted to imagine it as I believe it really would be. So I played the 'what if' game. What if you changed shape one day? Just shifted into something else? In this world—here, today. *Right now* while you're reading this. Look around you. How would people react if you were suddenly holding this page open with the claws and snout of a fox?

Ready to find out? Just sit back and enjoy the ride . . .

For Anna Farthing
(bringer of good and curious things)

OXFORD
UNIVERSITY PRESS

Great Clarendon Street, Oxford OX2 6DP
Oxford University Press is a department of the University of Oxford.
It furthers the University's objective of excellence in research, scholarship,
and education by publishing worldwide. Oxford is a registered trade mark of
Oxford University Press in the UK and in certain other countries

Copyright © Ali Sparkes 2016
The moral rights of the author have been asserted
Database right Oxford University Press (maker)
First published 2016

All rights reserved. No part of this publication may be reproduced,
stored in a retrieval system, or transmitted, in any form or by any means,
without the prior permission in writing of Oxford University Press,
or as expressly permitted by law, or under terms agreed with the appropriate
reprographics rights organization. Enquiries concerning reproduction
outside the scope of the above should be sent to the Rights Department,
Oxford University Press, at the address above
You must not circulate this book in any other binding or cover
and you must impose this same condition on any acquirer

British Library Cataloguing in Publication Data
Data available
ISBN: 978-0-19-274605-4

1 3 5 7 9 10 8 6 4 2
Printed in Great Britain
Paper used in the production of this book is a natural,
recyclable product made from wood grown in sustainable forests.
The manufacturing process conforms to the environmental
regulations of the country of origin.

THE SHAPESHIFTER

FEATHER AND FANG

ALI SPARKES

OXFORD
UNIVERSITY PRESS

The boy shivered. It was a cool night.

Also, he was stark naked.

But the goosebumps on his skin were nothing to do with the breeze. Nor was he troubled by being fully undressed outside. The trees and the low cloud across the moon cloaked him well and the press of twig and leaf into his bare soles was comforting.

What sent a chill through him was the thirty-second journey he was about to make. It would end in one of two ways:

1. Freedom
2. Death

Do you really need to do this? *asked a small, scared voice deep inside him.* Can't you just stay here and deal with it?

No, he told it. *No, he couldn't.*

He stared up at pale half-moonlit sky, framed in a circle of dark leaves; a well of light and space through the trees. Would this be the last time he stood in this wood? Would it be the last time he stood anywhere—ever?

A tawny owl called and its mate replied. Time was passing and this wouldn't get any easier for thinking about it. It really was now or never. Do or die.

With a rush of adrenalin and determination he shot up through the well in the canopy. He levelled off above the trees and began to fly in a wide arc around the handsome country house below.

He would miss this place. Desperately. But not quite enough to stay and live with what it had become.

He built up speed, circling the dark sky in a mile-wide radius.

It was nearly time. The vibrations of the dome were screaming in his brain now. Come on! COME ON! COME ON, SHAPESHIFTER! IF YOU THINK YOU'RE HARD ENOUGH!

He'd find out soon enough. If the calculations were wrong he would achieve freedom for about four seconds. Then they'd pick him off the fells and take him back to the lodge in plastic bags.

1

DOGGY DELIGHT AS DAISY 'WEDS' DIGBY

It was pooch picture perfect yesterday as reality TV star Jazzmeena staged a wedding ceremony for the little dog who's almost as famous as she is.

Daisy, the toy schizuana, who stands only fourteen centimetres high, was decked out in a diamond-studded tiara, matching collar, and white wedding veil as she was led to a pink marble altar to 'marry' Digby—a snow-white bichon frise.

'It was so sweet,' cooed Jazzmeena. 'Rev Spartacus, who was on *Celebrity Cellmates* with me, did such a lovely ceremony—and both doggies were so well-behaved. Daisy made such a beautiful bride.'

Two hundred celebrity guests were invited to the ceremony which was followed by a lavish reception at the twelve million pound mansion Jazzmeena shares with her five children and her fourth husband, cage-fighter Slap DeFace.

The only awkward moment was when Digby, resplendent in a golden waistcoat and a top hat, relieved himself on the

Caroline Fisher's fingers slowed to a halt. Slowly her head drooped. Oh God. The moment had come. Yup. It was officially here. The Moment When She Could Take No More.

Gbhbnjm,jnhbm,.jhmn,mkjmnkhbvgbhnjmk./„. leapt across the screen above as she headbutted the keyboard with low groans of defeat. It was finally over. She couldn't do this for *one more minute*.

After a decade as a reporter she should have been riding high by now. And for a while she was. She had been getting regular shifts at the *Independent* only last summer, working on hot political stories and some genuine investigative journalism. But plummeting newspaper sales and endless cutbacks had seen more and more freelancers laid off.

And now she was reduced to this. Working for the *Stand*: a tabloid paper she wouldn't even have lined a cat litter tray with this time last year.

She had told herself to get a grip. She *could* write the 'entertainment' section. She *could* do it. It was easy. It was just a way of earning money. She had a mortgage to pay on her little London flat. She COULD write stupid, vacuous celebrity stories. It wasn't going to kill her.

Except, maybe it was.

'Caroline.' A tap on the shoulder. She glanced around to see Archie, a fellow reporter. He grinned sympathetically.

'I told you you'd never last,' he said as she sat up. 'You're too good for this sleazy little rag.'

Caroline stood and picked up her bag. She would go and tell the editor now. This was it. Her career was officially over.

'Bye, Archie,' she said, with a rueful smile. She quite

liked Archie, even though he wrote the most awful tat in the place.

But before she could leave the newsroom there was a shout from Rick, the news editor. 'Oi! Fisher! Job for you.'

She shook her head. 'I'm done,' she said. 'Give it to Archie.'

'No—they're asking for you!' insisted Rick. 'Two girls down in reception. Wearing black veils. Probably a forced marriage story—get down there!'

Caroline winced. In the world of the *Stand*, girls in hijabs could only possibly have two stories attached to them—*forced marriage* or *suicide bomber*. A normal person underneath a hijab wasn't really what the *Stand* wrote about.

She closed her eyes for a few seconds and then decided she might as well talk to these girls before she left for ever—if only to convince them to take whatever story they had elsewhere.

They were sitting on a bench near the revolving door when she arrived. She walked over and introduced herself. 'Hi—I'm Caroline. You asked for me?' She scanned the girls' faces; what little she could see of them—and immediately realized something was off-kilter. They were wearing hijabs which covered their hair and most of their faces; long-sleeved cotton tops which fell to their hips; jeans and trainers beneath. It was the usual mash-up of traditional and modern which many westernized Muslims wore these days.

None of this was unusual in Tower Hamlets. Something *else* was. It was the girl on the right. Something about her manner was . . . off. The other one, dark-eyed and relaxed, fit her clothing with ease, but her friend . . . no. It didn't seem to sit right on her. The blue eyes were probably the clue—and a strand of dark blonde hair escaping the black cloth. Muslim white girls weren't unheard of, but . . .

'We wanted to talk to you,' said the blue-eyed one. She sounded young—maybe thirteen or fourteen. 'Alone.'

Caroline nodded. 'OK . . . there's an interview room just through here.' She indicated a door just behind the reception desk.

'Not here,' said the girl, with surprising firmness. 'Could be bugged.' Her dark-eyed friend turned and blinked at her. 'No, seriously,' she went on. 'It could. Don't you know *anything*? Over in the park is better.'

Intrigued and amused, Caroline followed them out through the revolving door and across to the small grassy area where local office workers took time out for lunch. It was just after eleven and almost deserted. They sat on a bench beneath a plane tree.

'Well . . . you have my attention,' said Caroline, fishing her notebook and pen out of her satchel. She smiled at them. 'So, what's all this about . . . er?'

'I'm Alice and she's Mina,' said the blue-eyed girl, nodding towards her friend. 'It's about my brother,' she went on. 'I think he's in danger.'

'OK . . .' said Caroline. For some reason her heartbeat was picking up a little. 'In what way in danger?'

'They're not letting him fly,' she said.

There was a long moment of silence. Caroline said nothing. Sometimes waiting was the best way. The blue-eyed girl simply stared back at her, tilting her head, waiting too.

'What's your surname?' asked Caroline, finally.

'Jones.'

Caroline felt the hairs on her arms and shoulders begin to prickle. 'OK, Alice Jones . . . and why would your brother need to fly?'

'Because he's Dax Jones. And if he can't fly . . . he'll die.'

Caroline felt the spin of the world slow down. Her skin was now completely awash with prickling. 'Alice,' she said, getting to her feet. 'Just give me two minutes to quit my job. Then I'm all yours . . .'

2

The body lay mangled on the grass; eyes glassy. It was obvious that the neck had snapped instantly. A head-on collision. Probably several other bones had shattered at the same time, judging by the spatters of blood across the torso. At least the victim wouldn't have known much about it.

'Please take note,' said Forrester. 'If you attempt to leave without permission, this could be you. The rules have changed.'

Dax Jones stared at the man.

'It's for your own safety,' the man said, widening his light grey eyes. 'You can still fly within the boundaries and as long as you're wearing your tracker chip, you should get a warning when you're close to the perimeter. You'll be safe. You'd be safer still if you would just agree to the chip under your skin.'

Dax said nothing. Chip or not, he knew when he was close to the perimeter; he could sense the weird vibrations. Most of the birds could too, which was why Forrester only had one paltry pigeon to show him. And for all Dax knew, that pigeon might just as easily have flown into a closed window. He wouldn't put it past Forrester to relocate the body, just to make his point. Still, he wasn't about to say any of this.

'So remember, if you wish to go outside the boundaries, all you have to do is apply for permission, just as the other COLAs do,' the man said, with a tight, self-satisfied smile. 'One rule for everyone. It's perfectly fair. I'm sure you'll agree.'

'Are you?' said Dax but Forrester had already turned away and was stalking back to Fenton Lodge.

Silently, Dax shifted into a fox and slid away into the woods. He had done it hundreds, maybe thousands of times by now but he still felt the relief that this—his first shapeshift form—always brought him. He sometimes worried that maybe his *real* form was a fox and the boy form was the temporary one. If he didn't care so much about other humans in his world he might simply remain a fox for life. The lake he was skirting reflected russet-red fur, a white throat, and fine black whiskers; his legs and paws darkening from red to almost-black. It was five years since he'd first shifted and there was nothing cub-like about him any more. But that didn't mean he wasn't sometimes as scared as a cub.

He still had nearly half the perimeter to check. If he was right . . . and he very much feared he was . . . the entire Fenton Lodge estate was now sealed. Work had been going on for weeks—diggers and pile drivers and specialist equipment and crew had created a cast iron perimeter. It rose four metres above the ground, dwarfing the old stone walls on the outer side. The barrier sank four metres below too. They'd sliced through earth, stones, and tree roots and driven the metal down with mechanical ferocity and precision. As a dog-fox he could dig . . . but he wasn't a *mole*. He couldn't dig *that* far down and they knew it.

And the flying option was now sealed off too.

He met Gideon by the river. His friend was pacing the bank and skimming several stones across the water in small telekinetic spasms. He dropped them all as soon as Dax arrived, skirting the fence, sharp dark nose to the ground. Dax paused at the water's edge. This part of the perimeter was the worst. Instead of the beautiful view of the river cascading down through the Cumbrian valley, there was now a wall of iron. Where it met the water, it became a grid—a portcullis dropped through the shining current. A few weeks ago there had been just a high brick wall on either side of the river and some near-invisible mesh fence. The mesh had been electrified, of course, but even so—there had been a normal view. A glimpse of the world beyond the estate.

Today there was just a sliver of view a few centimetres above the water and that was chopped up like a line of kitchen tiles framed in iron.

'Have you tried this bit yet?' asked Gideon, rubbing his hand through his messy blond hair and grimacing at the portcullis.

Dax shifted directly to otter and slipped into the river with barely a splash. He dived down and followed the current into the darker depths, streaming green and brown weed caressing his sleek fur. A few metres along he slammed up against the iron grid. Following the metal struts downward with his snout and forepaws he found they were driven deep into the river bed. The area was still churned up and silty from the violent work of the specialized construction crew. Fish could slide on through the gaps but Dax, even as a sinewy and agile otter, could not. They had calculated the dimensions with care. He was caged.

Back on the bank he shook water from his pelt and then shifted back to boy form, on hands and knees, staring grimly into the river.

'All the way down?' asked Gideon. Dax nodded. This is bad,' said the telekinetic. His green eyes looked bleak and shadowed. He scanned the wall of iron with a scowl. 'I could rip that apart, if you like.'

Dax nodded. 'I know you could,' he said, getting to his feet. 'But then what? If you—and Lisa and Luke and everyone—could shapeshift like me, we could all be out of here seconds after you'd done it. But you can't. You can't get away. They monitor everything. They'll know the moment you try to flex your telly skills and they'll be waiting for you on the other side.'

'*You* could get out,' mumbled Gideon, unhappily.

'And leave everyone I care about behind?' snapped Dax.

'Not everyone . . . Owen and Tyrone are still out there,' said Gideon, gazing out across the top of the wall. 'You could get to Spain and find them.'

Dax eyed the sky and saw a different place in his mind; the gold, red, and green shades of a Spanish mountainside with a distant sea view. Owen and Tyrone had once worked as teachers and mentors with the COLAs here at Fenton Lodge. To get away, one of them had had to 'die'—at least as far as the British government was concerned. Now Owen and Ty lived deep in a cave system where no surveillance tech or psychic dowser could find them. That was what it took to stay free . . . and Dax knew he could join them any time he wanted. He felt a pull inside him. Owen meant as much to Dax as Gideon and Lisa. He loved Owen as much—maybe even more than—his father, and the weeks he had spent believing the man was dead had ripped him apart. Finding Owen again had been the most emotional moment of his life. So yes . . . Gideon *could* get him out and he would have a place to go. On his own.

'It's not an option,' said Dax. 'Not now. Come on. Let's stop moping about it. We might as well go back and have tea.' He trudged off towards the lodge and Gideon followed him in silence.

Dax could have told Gideon about the magnetic dome and Forrester's threats, but what was the point? The dome would freak him out. He'd get mad and maybe drop a brick wall on Forrester next time he saw him. And then what? Gideon would be overpowered sooner or later—shot, maybe. And if he survived he'd be in lockdown . . . perhaps for ever.

And anyway, Dax wasn't convinced the dome *could* hold him. It wasn't *actually* a force field, after all, but a field of magnetic resonance which messed with a bird's navigational cortex in the brain and caused instant, nauseating disorientation. He knew this. He'd already flown through it. A few days ago Forrester had collected him for an outdoors *Development* session and taken him to the far side of the copse. Here in a remote clearing they'd set up a pair of metal towers, each of which stood on a heavy wheeled base and rose about three metres high. Forrester had told him that the towers, the markers along the grass, and the research assistants with clipboards and cameras, were there to test Dax's speed and agility.

Dax had not been fooled for a second. The frequency of the magnetic field, pulsating invisibly between the two metal rigs, was thrumming in his ears the moment he cleared the trees, still in boy form. Most of his animal senses worked even when he wasn't feathered or furry.

But he had pretended to be fooled. As soon as he'd met Forrester he had scented a foe. The man was all about control and the one thing he could not stand was a student who wouldn't be tamed. A free pass to fly around the estate had been Dax's privilege for some years now. The staff at the school understood it was essential for his health. Even a part-time falcon needed to fly and the scientists knew this. But Forrester was not happy. Not happy at all. Especially when Dax refused to have the tracking chip inserted under his skin. Some of the more biddable COLAs and their families had been talked into it recently. But when it came to the Shapeshifter, it was not so easy. A signed consent from Dax's father was necessary and Dax knew Robert Jones would never give it without his son's agreement.

So Forrester's latest attempt to contain him came as no surprise—but Dax had needed to know what his new enemy had lined up for him so he did as he was asked. He flew, low and slow, through the field and in seconds he was tumbling to Earth, dazed and sick. The smug look on Forrester's thin face and the congratulatory smiles he got from the two scientists with him, made Dax want to drive his talons into the man's throat. But he was in no fit state. It took him several minutes to recover enough to stand. Later, Forrester had summoned him and told him about the dome. This morning's dead pigeon stunt was a little reminder. As if he needed any reminding when cast iron walls were being built around him.

'They're turning this place into a prison,' said Gideon, as if he was reading Dax's mind as they trudged back to the lodge. 'I hate to admit it . . . but Spook was right.'

Dax didn't answer. He wanted to keep Gideon calm. Yes, their old enemy—COLA Club's most powerful and arrogant illusionist—had had it nailed. That's why Spook had escaped a year ago, casually leaving devastation in his wake. But if Fenton Lodge—the school and home they had grown to love over the past few years—was being turned into a prison, not everyone here knew it yet. It was a beautiful prison and at first glance no more secure than any expensive boarding school; the kind of place the offspring of a billionaire or a high-ranking government minister might attend. At second glance, the high walls and electronic gates might intrigue an outsider. A third glance at the discreetly armed soldiers stationed at every access point would probably excite a bit more interest. But as it was in such a remote part of the Lake District, very few people ever *would* glance even once. The farmers in the area had all been paid off to remain tight-lipped about anything they saw—as had the families of Fenton Lodge's one hundred or so students.

And the truth was, the families *wanted* to believe that everything was fine. After all, if your child was a freak of nature, wouldn't you want to believe they were somewhere secure? However much you loved them? A Child Of Limitless Ability gave a whole new meaning to the title 'special needs'. The freaks of nature at Fenton Lodge, or COLA Club as the students themselves called it, could do all kinds of amazing things.

Terrifying things too.

3

The Children of Limitless Ability Project
Categories A, B, & C
Risk appraisal

Category C
This group contains telepaths, psychics, mediums, clairvoyants, clairaudients, dowsers, and healers.

RISK: *Low.* These COLAs represent no known physical danger to staff or public with the exception of one healer, Mia Cooper—who is no longer with the Project. Healers are Cat. C pending any behaviour which may lead to Cat. B or higher.

Category B
This group contains glamourists—including those with powers of illusion, vanishing (also known as cloaking), mimicry, and shapeshifting.

RISK: *Moderate.* While no more able to inflict physical harm than a normal teenager, this group can affect the well-being of staff or public by creating fear, panic, confusion, and misdirection. The shapeshifter is capable of attack with animal speed and strength (but has no history of this on staff or public).

Category A

This group contains telekinetics, pyrokinetics, and teleporters. At present the Project has only telekinetics.

RISK: *High.* There is no history of violence among the telekinetics but their powers are potentially life-threatening on a large scale. High-end demonstrations include holding back tidal waters and falling cliff faces, as well as overturning an armoured coach, bending metal, and slowing the speed of a bullet. All of these actions were retrospectively sanctioned by the COLA Project as necessary, and indeed life-saving, at the time of use. However, the potential risk remains. And it is, as the Project title reminds us, *limitless.*

Note: Many COLAs have more than one talent. Their highest risk talent will define their category. We currently have no pyrokinetic or teleporter COLAs within the Project. See files on Mia Cooper and Olu Jackson.

Footnote: Only one Fenton Lodge student is uncategorized in terms of ability. Clive Smith is our control student, having no COLA talent. As he spends much of his time with Barry Blake (glamourist) and occasionally Dax Jones (shapeshifter), we have placed him in Cat. B for convenience.

The Categories came in days after Forrester took over from David Chambers as head of the COLA Project. They weren't meant to be known to the COLAs but it was just a matter of time—hours—before it got out. The students weren't stupid and quite a lot of them were psychic. It caused some mild controversy as everyone jostled to find out what category they were in. Some were relieved to be in Cat. C. Some were annoyed not to be in Cat. B or Cat. A.

Dax didn't want to be in any category but it disturbed him that his best friend was in Cat. A while he was in Cat. B.

Gideon, though, seemed to find the whole thing hilarious.

'What's Lisa Hardman doing in Cat. C?' he snorted. 'With all the other wifty-wafties? Don't they know how dangerous she is? That girl has sulks of mass destruction.'

It was true that Lisa had been in a very bad mood for a long time now. And she never really had fitted in with the other healers, psychics, and other 'wifty-wafties,' as Gideon always called them. The Project's most talented psychic medium, telepath, and dowser had never been grateful for her 'gifts' to start with. And with the ceaseless onslaught of dead people who tried to communicate through her, day and night, it wasn't hard to see why. 'Give her a break, Gid,' Dax said. 'She misses Mia.'

'We all miss Mia,' Gideon said.

'Yeah, but—they were best mates.'

Gideon shrugged. 'We're Lisa's mates too.'

'Do you talk to her about make-up? Boys? Bad hair days?'

Gideon shuddered. 'Point taken.'

Gideon was also amazed that others had got as high

as Cat. B. 'Barry Blake?' he scoffed. 'You're kidding me.' Barry was a glamourist whose speciality was turning himself invisible. He and his friend, Jennifer Troke— another vanisher—were learning tae kwon do. Barry—big and stocky—was doing his best but small, lithe Jennifer was way ahead of him. 'Seriously, you wouldn't mess with Jennifer,' Gideon said, 'but Barry, he's the Pie Ninja.'

Most of Barry's talent *was* deployed in pursuit of pastries from the Fenton Lodge kitchens. And even that wasn't too successful since Mrs P. had learned to fling a handful of flour at any suspicious noises in the vicinity, instantly revealing their shape in white powder. 'Seriously,' said Gideon, 'what kind of superpower gets defeated by Homepride self-raising?!'

Gideon had no quarrel with himself and his twin brother, Luke, being placed in Cat. A. They were the most powerful telekinetics in the COLA Club. Probably in the world. The pair of them had gone through some scary stuff over the past few years and they were under no illusions about how dangerous their powers could be. They had learned to play it all down but nobody was likely to forget the things they had done. If the COLA Project psychologists ever picked up anything other than the decent, open-hearted characters they were, they'd be in trouble.

The only other brothers in COLA Club were Alex and Jacob Teller. They were Cat. B. Their mimicry skills were so incredible they could do serious damage to voice-activated security. Their audio glamour had caused mayhem last summer—but they too were solid and decent and all the psych tests suggested they were loyal to the Project and not a danger to it.

For some time after Forrester had arrived there had been no reason to be troubled. Nothing much changed. Nobody saw much of the new man in charge and school life went on as before. Then the diggers arrived to make the perimeter 'more safe' and Fenton Lodge began to feel a little less like home.

'Dax, what are we going to do?' asked Gideon, breaking into his friend's melancholy train of thought. They were sitting on the steps of the lodge—a stately building of warm golden sandstone with a whitewashed façade and tall Georgian windows at the front. It was flanked by numerous modern wings and outbuildings to accommodate the 109 students and a team of teachers, scientists, and security specialists.

'I don't know yet,' said Dax.

'Maybe it'll calm down. Maybe Chambers will come back,' said Gideon. 'Or maybe the families will start to kick up about the new rules. They're meant to be consulted, aren't they? I've written to Dad about it.'

Dax bit back the words forming on his tongue. He'd been about to say 'Gideon, you idiot! Do you really think your letters are reaching your dad just the way you sent them?!' but something in his friend's face told him to stop. Gideon still had hope.

'I wrote to mine too,' he said, instead. 'And to Alice.'

Gideon snorted. 'To Alice? What—to complain about

the metal walls and the tracker chips and all that?! And get the considered insights of a thirteen-year-old girl?'

Dax grinned. 'No,' he admitted. 'Not that.'

'What then?'

'I wrote to her about *Celebrity Cellmates*.'

'Yeah,' said Gideon, getting up and heading in through the main entrance. 'Sure you did.'

The cameras over the doorway moved fluidly to track their progress, and behind the huge gilded mirror in the hall, the directors, producers, and floor managers of their world worked in silence.

Dax waved at them. They hated it when he did that.

4

Dear Alice,

Life goes on much the same at Fenton Lodge. Me and Gid have been trying to build another deck on the tree house and Gid's lost two fingernails so far. He's still really bad with a hammer. We've finished our GCSEs now and can chill out for the summer.

How's life with you? Are you learning much at your posh school? Thanks for the photos of you and Dad. Could you BE more fake tanned? And doesn't that sparkly stuff get in your eyes? You look like that pop star—Jazzmeena, is it?—on *Celebrity Cellmates*. She had sparkly stuff stuck all over her orange face when she was voted out. Just promise me you won't ever get surgery like that. Gid reckons several people could probably survive at sea by hanging on to her implants. Do you think she and Slap DeFace will make it? You have to hope this marriage will work, for the sake of all those kids. Loved the Rebel Rev. as well—the one who had to preach a sermon while getting a high-pressure hose full of custard down his trousers. Reality TV, eh? You gotta love it. Imagine having everything you do watched, though . . . and not being allowed to go out. Still, it would be worth it to be famous, wouldn't it? Hope you can come up to the fell cottages with Dad soon.

Love Dax

Caroline put the letter down on the cafe table. Alice raised her eyebrows. They were now fully in view, shaded slightly by the pink felt beanie hat.

'OK,' said Caroline. 'So . . . he's got into reality TV and has an unhealthy fixation on a pop star's boobs. He's sixteen—what do you expect?'

Alice rolled her eyes. 'Seriously?! Do you KNOW Dax?'

Caroline considered this. Did she? It had been years since she'd met the boy, and although they'd kept in touch the letters were very occasional. A few times she had applied to meet with him at the new college he was at in Cumbria—via the official channels—but had never been granted access.

'He HATES reality TV!' said Alice. 'He has NEVER watched *Celebrity Cellmates*! NEVER! Until now, obviously . . . because, yeah, that Slap DeFace guy is bad news and Jazz should really kick him out. He's a love rat! She should dump him YESTERDAY!'

Caroline paused to weigh up this vision of teenage in front of her. The pink hat, the ludicrous load of gloss on lip, the mass of friendship bracelets, the sparkly pink bobbles at the end of each plait, and the sequinned 'BABE' across her pink T-shirt were all at complete odds with what had occurred in Alice Jones's world over the past hour.

They had arranged to meet again at a cafe in a nearby shopping centre. The girls had both arrived in hijabs as before and then, as Caroline waited bemused at the table, had walked straight to the ladies' toilets at the back of the premises.

Five minutes later they'd come back out and left the cafe without so much as a glance at her. A minute after that, a skinny girl in pink had come out of the toilets and sat down in front of her. Alice had pulled off an impressive switcheroo. Another school friend, it emerged, had gone into the toilets a minute or two ahead of them—and when Alice and Mina had arrived, the other girl had taken on the veil and left again with Mina. Alice had breezed back out a minute later, every inch the modern western girl.

Caroline didn't ask why. She could guess. Anyone connected with a COLA was under surveillance; some more than others. She herself had been tracked for a long time and only in the last year or so had she thought that maybe the government wasn't bothering any more. Now she wasn't so sure. She was impressed that Alice had worked it out, though. Even more impressed by how she had got around it . . . assuming she *had*.

But this letter? She sighed. 'Alice—what do *you* think Dax is trying to tell you?'

'Isn't it obvious?' Alice slurped some smoothie and rolled her eyes again. 'And you're supposed to be an investigative reporter!'

'Not any more,' said Caroline. 'Just quit, remember?'

'Look!' Alice pointed to a line in Dax's scrawly hand: *Imagine having everything you do watched, though . . . and not being allowed to go out. Still, it would be worth it to be famous, wouldn't it?*

Caroline felt foolish. The one thing she most definitely remembered about Dax was that he was the last boy in the world to want to be famous. The girl was right. The letter was weird. It was sending a whole other message. *Imagine having everything you do watched, though . . . and not being allowed to go out.* It couldn't be much plainer, could it?

'You think he's being held against his will?' she said, quietly—acutely aware of the other diners now.

Alice nodded. 'He was always allowed to fly,' she said, in a low voice. 'Because when they tried to stop him he had . . . a kind of stroke thing. He nearly died. He has to be able to fly. And that meant they couldn't keep him in.

They could keep all the others in but not Dax. They just had to trust him.'

Caroline closed her eyes for a moment. She had seen Dax Jones shift to a fox and back again. But she had never seen him take the form of a peregrine falcon. Although he'd told her about it in his letters, there was still something in her sceptical journalist's brain which rebelled against such an idea. How could that *be*? Somehow, shifting to a mammal, not much smaller than Dax himself when she had met him, was something her logical brain could just about wrap itself around. But a bird? A small, feathered thing? Where did all that body mass go? How could it just contract and twist into so utterly changed a thing? And then FLY?

'Have you seen it?' she asked, softly.

Alice shrugged and slurped more smoothie through the straw like a six-year-old. 'Seen what?'

'Have you seen him shift . . . into a fox or a bird or . . . ?'

'An otter?' asked Alice. 'No—not an otter—but the fox and the bird, yeah. He went mental with my mum a couple of years ago and shifted right in front of her for the first time. It was scary. Fox—all teeth and growling. Bird—all swoopy and scratchy talons. I nearly wet myself. But I had seen him being a fox before anyway, way back when I was a kid. When he was still at home with us.'

'Really?'

'Yeah—I thought maybe I'd dreamed it but then I realized it was real. There were fox paw prints on the

floor. He cleaned them up later but I saw them. But . . .
I didn't say anything. It was too weird. And Mum would
have gone totally batsh—totally mad.'

'So . . . she and Dax . . . they still don't get on?'

'No. She thinks he's a mutant alien freak-job,' grinned
Alice. 'She doesn't want him in the house. He never came
home again after he showed her the true him.'

'What about your dad . . . he's an oil rig worker, yes?'

'Yeah—so he comes home, but if he wants to see Dax
he has to go and stay in the little cottages they have up
there on the estate. They're lovely. I want to go again but
Mum hasn't let me. She thinks I might get . . . infected.'
For a moment her eyes shone. 'Do you think I could
be . . . infected?'

Caroline smiled and shook her head. 'I think Dax's
talents came down from his birth mother . . . not from
your dad.'

'Shame,' sighed Alice. 'I'd love to be able to fly. But . . .
then I guess if I could I'd be locked up in the middle of
nowhere too.'

Caroline took a deep breath. 'Alice—why did you
come to me with this? Is there something you think I
can do? I mean . . . why not go to your dad?'

Alice shrugged. 'Dad's away. He's nearly always away.
And he just says things like "the government people know
what they're doing" and "he's in the best place" like he's
in some kind of mental hospital or dead or something.
And Dax has sent his message to *me*—not anyone else.
He thinks I'm the one who might help.'

A little flicker of pride passed across her face and Caroline suddenly realized that Alice *idolized* her big brother. Wow. Who would have thought it? An idea suddenly occurred to her. Not a welcome one. 'Alice . . . have you told your friends about Dax? Mina . . . and the other girl who helped you today? What do they know?'

Alice fixed her with steady eyes. 'I'm not *stupid*. They don't know anything. They just think Dax is at a posh boarding school . . . and the school has taken his passport away and won't let him fly abroad. Because he looks like a terrorist.'

Caroline blinked. Was looking mixed-race all it took these days? 'But you said, in front of Mina, that he'll die if he can't fly.'

'Yeah—he's mad about travelling the world!' said Alice, her voice rising and becoming melodramatic and sulky. 'And if they won't let him be free he'll just DIE!' She took a breath and had another shot of smoothie. 'That's what I told them,' she said, back in a normal tone. 'What can I say? I'm a total drama queen.'

Caroline laughed and shook her head. Alice Jones was much, much sharper than she would have guessed. 'OK—I get it. But even so, what made you think of coming to me?'

Alice flipped up her palms. 'The power of the press!' she said. 'You do a big story on it and make them come clean about what's really going on up there!'

Caroline smiled sadly. *Oh dear.* 'Alice—I think you overestimate my powers. The COLA Project is one of the most powerful forces in this country. The people who run it—they answer to nobody but the Prime Minister and they have incredible resources. How do you think stories about the COLA Project haven't got out into the mainstream media already? Not because there isn't loads of eyewitness evidence. I've been tracking it on social media as far as I can but there's really very little being reported and most people think it's nonsense— conspiracy theory twaddle. Why? Because it's all getting hushed up as soon as it happens. All the top dogs in the media are getting told or bribed or warned to stay away from it. If I even attempted to talk to a newspaper editor about Dax, it would get back to the COLA Project in a matter of minutes. And then they'd be coming after me to shut me down.'

Alice's eyes went round. 'Shut you down? You mean they'd . . .'

'Not to kill me,' said Caroline, quickly. 'There are other ways to mess up a person's life. Like having their bank accounts frozen and all their family's credit cards stopped. Maybe arresting them on suspicion of terrorist activities. Easy, Alice. Really easy.' Caroline thought about the evidence she had secretly been gathering over the past few years. She had no intention of using it to advance her career . . . it was now an insurance policy to protect her life. A few keystrokes on a laptop could blow the COLA Project wide open but she hoped she'd never have to do it. She didn't mention this to Alice. The kid was scared enough already.

'But—*we* all know about the COLAs,' said Alice. 'All their families—so how come . . . ?'

'How is your lovely new house?' asked Caroline. She remembered the dingy terraced place Dax had been living at when she'd first doorstepped him. She would bet big money that Alice and her mother no longer lived there.

'It's . . . great,' said Alice. Realization was dawning across her young face.

'And your lovely posh school? Good, is it?'

Alice shook her head, a frown creasing her young brow beneath the pink hat. 'Dad got promoted—he got more money at work.'

'Is that right? Do you really think that he got soooo promoted that you could suddenly move in to a five bedroom house in Rich Toffsville and then magically go to a fee-paying independent school along with the sons and daughters of foreign diplomats and TV presenters?'

Alice looked at her glittery fingernails and said nothing for a few seconds. She coloured up a little. Eventually she mumbled: 'I'm stupid, aren't I? I never worked it out.'

'That there was hush money?' Caroline patted her hand. 'Look—you were only a kid. Why wouldn't you believe what they told you? And it's not like you're alone. Every close family member of a COLA is getting paid to keep quiet. It was the policy. What else could they do? Bang you all up in a giant concrete bunker so you'd never tell? Hundreds of people?'

Alice didn't say anything. She looked deflated and suddenly much younger than her thirteen years.

'You're not stupid, Alice,' said Caroline. 'You're a very smart girl. I mean, you worked out that you were most likely being kept under surveillance, didn't you? That hijab switch stunt was pretty cool. So . . . let's bring it back to the main question. What can I do to help? Practically?'

Alice looked up at her. 'I don't know.'

'Nor do I,' said Caroline. 'But I think it's time to find out.'

5

'Brilliant! Another dead kid. Just what I was hoping for.'

Dax and Gideon found Lisa in the common room, sitting at a leather-topped table, filling out SCN slips. Her head was bowed over the little pile of pink tickets. Her hair, cut into a sharp, shiny bob, was the colour of a wheat field in August but nothing else about her was sunny.

'Lisa Hardman—angel to the bereft and suffering,' said Gideon, brightly.

She glared up and he and Dax immediately stepped back. Her dark blue eyes were opaque and this meant she was only half in their world. The other half of her was—very reluctantly—in someone else's. If Dax went up and touched her shoulder he might get a glimpse of what her psychic mind was experiencing. He did not plan to do this. Being a part-time animal meant he had acquired some simple telepathic skills and the very talented COLA psychics could transmit to him. But getting into Lisa's head these days was usually a grim thing. She was unhappy and it seemed the spirit world was homing in on this with alarming enthusiasm. She was getting some pretty nasty visions, premonitions and messages—24/7.

Fortunately, they were all meant for other people

and Lisa was merely the channel. It was her job to fill out Spirit Communication Notices and pass them on to Control – the COLA Project's ever present team of advisors and decision makers. It was part of Control's job to track down any living people involved and pass the messages along to them—or to the police. Full of detail and sometimes even map reference points, Lisa's SCN slips were sad but precious gifts from the great hereafter. Murder and missing persons investigations across the UK had become a little easier since Lisa's COLA talent had been discovered. The source of the tip-offs was never revealed or pursued. Lisa worked on without help, hindrance, or congratulation.

And on most days, without any enthusiasm. She hated being the Call Centre for the Great Hereafter. Watching her now; her thin shoulders hunched and her fists clenched, Dax wished for the one hundredth time that he could help her the way Mia had. Mia had always known what to do to ease Lisa's stress. Dax couldn't match it. Even so, he glanced at Gideon.

Gideon nodded. 'Yeah, mate,' he said. 'Do the furry thing.'

Dax shifted and went to sit next to Lisa. He made no sound other than the gentle clipping of his neat black claws on the woodblock flooring. He curled his tail across his forepaws and waited beside her chair. Thirty seconds later, Lisa instinctively unclenched her left fist and allowed it to snake down and stroke the thick red fur across Dax's head and shoulders. He could hear her heart rate ease as she made the connection with him. He didn't say anything. Flashes of Lisa's current spirit communication were crackling across to his mind from hers, like static. A kid—about eight or nine—dead in a chalk pit somewhere in Wales. A murder? No. A horrible, hapless accident. Other kids had run away, too scared to tell anyone what had happened—the knock-on misery would spread like a shockwave through dozens and dozens of families, just as soon as Lisa had dowsed the exact location and passed the information up the line.

The weight of this sadness was already dragging him down and once again he was reminded why Lisa was so hard and shiny about this stuff. How could she not be? If you were even slightly porous—if only ten per cent of all this seeped into you—you'd never get out of bed again.

Lisa scribbled a location on the SCN slip and then slapped it down on the pile.

Dax nudged her hand with his snout. *Stop now*.

She sat up straight and looked around at him. Her eyes looked normal again. 'Yeah,' she said. 'I'm shutting up shop for the day.'

Dax shifted back to boy form and Gideon wandered across. 'Why are you doing SCN slips up here and not down in Development?' Gideon asked. 'You should come up here and chill.'

'Chill?' she said and fixed him with a stare that could freeze a polar bear.

'He means you need a place to relax,' said Dax. 'And that's what the common room is meant to be.' He glanced around at the large room with its tall windows and assorted leather or red brocade sofas, grouped around low tables. There were four or five other COLAs at the far end, watching the flat-screen TV, but most were still in Development sessions, outside in the grounds, or off in their own rooms.

Lisa let out a long breath and stretched. Even tired and dishevelled, she still looked good in her pale-green sweater and her expensive designer jeans. 'I don't like the Development rooms. I told them I get a better signal up here.'

Gideon snorted. 'A better signal? What—like Wi-Fi? And they bought that?!'

Lisa gave him a look. '*They* don't know the difference,' she muttered, keeping her voice low. 'I just get sick of being watched all the time.'

'You're being watched here too, you know,' said Gideon, flicking a glance at the security cameras tucked discreetly into each corner of the wood-panelled walls.

'I know,' she said. 'I'm not an idiot. I just *feel* less watched up here. Without those stupid giant two-way mirrors they have downstairs.'

'To be honest, Lees,' said Dax, sitting down on the couch opposite, next to Gideon. 'They're probably not watching you half as much as you think they are. You're only Cat. C, remember. You don't freak them out like Gideon does.'

'Yeah—you're boring, you are,' said Gideon. 'What are they going to see? Your grumpy little face and a lot of stroppy scribbling, that's what. They must draw straws to see who has to do Cat. C spying duty. Half of them are probably asleep behind that mirror.'

Lisa gave him a sour look. As reluctant as she was to fulfil her duties, Lisa had a massive ego. Being possibly the most talented psychic medium and dowser in the world, she did not appreciate being referred to as anything less than grade A. Dax often wondered what she would do if someone ever found a way to 'cure' her of her 'gift'. Would she accept the cure and go back to her pampered princess lifestyle with her rich daddy? He wasn't sure.

'I need a break,' she said. 'A holiday. A real one.'

They nodded. Everyone felt the same. The closely watched leisure time they got with families in the cottages up on the fells wasn't a real holiday. Not for them. The families usually loved it—the cottages were luxuriously fitted out. Five star. There were hot tubs and home cinemas and gorgeous views in the lovely stone cottages. There were healthy walks with stunning scenery and fascinating wildlife. There was excellent food from the Fenton Lodge kitchens and a maid service to keep everything looking perfect. But there wasn't any freedom. Not for the COLAs, anyway.

Over the years, trips home had been become less and less frequent and ever more tightly controlled, especially for the Cat. As. The COLAs at Fenton Lodge barely noticed the microscopic tracker chips in their clothes and shoes these days. But Dax could never forget; the connection between the chips and the tracking equipment back at base gave out a high frequency which he could always detect, even when he was in boy form. It ran day and night. He had learned to tune it out up to a point but it still nagged at his senses. The chips in his clothes and shoes somehow still worked when he was in another form. His outerwear, within his field of life-force (what the healers would call his 'aura') shifted with him, morphing to fur or feather. This had saved him from much embarrassment in life. He didn't have to re-enter his boy form stark naked. But sometimes, when he was quite alone, he would go deep into the little wood near the lodge and strip off completely. Then he would shift into a falcon, a fox, or an otter, and be truly free of the tagging. He was careful not to abuse this freedom; he knew if he took it too far—went off grid for too long and caused concern—there would be consequences.

'Anyway—you're getting the retreat, aren't you?' Gideon was saying. 'Tomorrow. You get to go to some fancy spa hotel place in Dorset and ponce about in dressing gowns and get massages and scented candles and the full wifty-wafty, don't you?'

Lisa made a growling noise.

Gideon chortled. 'You'll LOVE it! All those psychics and telepaths and healers opening their chakras and sharing their chi!'

'Do you *want* a slap, Reader?' she snapped. Lisa was the least wifty-wafty COLA in existence. She had no patience at all for any of the New Age stuff that came with the other Cat. Cs. Most of them were gentle souls and, if truth be told, a few were . . . drippy. The ones with the least talent seemed to be the drippiest. Probably because it was easy to see psychic mediumship, dowsing, and healing as a 'gift' if your ability was so mild you never really got the full on nasty stuff like Lisa did.

Mia had been pretty wifty-wafty, though, remembered Dax. And there was nothing drippy about her the last time he'd seen her.

'Well, at least you'll get out!' Gideon was saying. 'You'll get a coach trip and a change of scene and yeah, sure, they'll track you and spy on you and probably try to inject some kind of tracking fluid into your aura while you're asleep but hey—different food!'

'Gid—you're really not helping,' said Dax, laughing. 'It will be a change, though, won't it, Lees?'

Lisa shook back her hair and closed her eyes briefly. 'Why don't they just let me go home? I could be riding round the estate and *really* relaxing instead of floating in a Jacuzzi, fending off endless offers of bloody reiki!'

Dax sighed. It would be a lot easier if Lisa had made friends with some of the other Cat. Cs but she wouldn't. She was stuck up and distant with them. Although all the others were in awe of her abilities, none of them much wanted to hang around with her.

'Anyway,' Lisa said, getting up. 'I'm going to start packing. I might as well look good while I'm hanging out with the duds.'

'Lisa!' Dax shook his head. 'They are *not* duds! Some of them are really good now. I mean . . . nowhere near as good as you but that's hardly their fault, is it?'

She shrugged, gathering her SCN slips in a tight bundle. 'Trust me—they don't *want* to be as talented as I am. It's no picnic. You're better off a dud.'

A couple of the COLAs down the far end of the room glanced away from the TV and back at them.

'Keep your voice down!' said Gideon. 'You're your own worst enemy, you are.'

Lisa tilted her head to one side, with a swing of golden hair across her jaw. 'Seriously, Gid? Even if I don't say DUD out loud, half of them can mind read just well enough to hear it SCREAMING in my head!' She smirked at him.

He rolled his eyes as she stalked away. 'You are *never* going to get another girl pal with that mouth, sister.'

'I don't want one,' she said, and the door slammed shut behind her.

'I won't miss her,' said Gideon.

'Yeah you will,' replied Dax. 'Where will you be without Hardman to torment for two weeks?'

'She doesn't know when she's well off; getting a spa break holiday,' muttered Gideon. 'Why don't we get a spa break holiday? Why can't I have hot stones laid on my back by a beautiful woman in a white tunic?'

'Dream on,' said Dax.

'I could stow away on the coach; go with them—sneak in and pretend to be a wifty-wafty,' Gid went on.

'You'd have to be a naked wifty-wafty,' Dax pointed out. 'Tracker chips!'

'OK—so I could steal one of the soldier's outfits and—'

'Just stay here,' said Dax. Gideon glanced over, picking up the serious tone. Dax shrugged. *He* didn't know what he meant either; except that everything was getting weird and he needed Gideon to be steady.

And something about Lisa's spa trip was bothering him. Something he couldn't put a finger on. Or a claw . . . or a talon.

6

The *Duchess of the Thames* lay in a quiet, sheltered dock. Her sister, the *Countess of the Thames*, was out cruising but the *Duchess* was unchartered today.

The empty pleasure craft rose and fell gently with the water, her wooden upper deck warm in the afternoon sun. A butterfly flew over the buddleia bushes which sprawled across one end of the dock in a tangled tapestry of green and purple. It landed on the cabin's metal roof and opened its wings to bask in the heat.

Until a shockwave blew it sideways across the deck.

Two figures stepped into view from nowhere. One, a skinny boy with dreadlocks and attitude; the other a tall, slim, dark-haired girl who stood in the epicentre of the shockwave with a smile like the Mona Lisa—as if punching a hole through the laws of physics was nothing unusual.

The girl crouched down, causing her long white leather coat to creak gently, and ran slender fingers across the bleached planks of the deck.

She stood again; walked along with soft clicks of her high-heeled white boots. She paused to touch the crushed butterfly and send it flitting back to the buddleia blooms. Then she leant on the brass guard rail at the aft of the vessel, gazing across the quiet stretch of river.

After a long, contented breath she turned to the boy. In the centre of the deck, he was bouncing in his trainers; as agitated as she was calm. When she fixed her violet eyes on his face, he fell still and shoved his hands into his jeans pockets. 'Well?' he said. 'Will it do?'

She smiled and goosebumps rose visibly on his arms. 'It will,' she said. Her voice was as cool and soft as a forest stream. 'It's perfect. Well done.'

'Great . . . so, we get this one?' he asked, beginning to bounce again. 'On the same day St. Evangeline's go out on the other? We'll book it online, yeah? Then . . .'

'Relax,' she said. 'It'll be taken care of.'

He relaxed, but only a bit. 'It's a lot of risk,' he said. 'Just to get your mates out. What if they don't want to come?'

'They will,' said Mia, although there was a flicker of uncertainty in her eyes. 'Once they really understand what's happening. And once they know we have taken control of the Prime Minister.'

The boy watched the gentle tide for a few seconds before speaking again. 'But if we just did one little kidnap . . . you could keep the kid happy and not freak out the rest and still get the PM—'

'It needs to be more public. More of a spectacle,' said the girl.

'But, y'know—little kids,' he shook his head. 'They'll be scared. I mean, they're just kids aren't they?' He shrugged and looked down at his feet.

'We're all just kids,' she said. 'That's the point.'

She took his hand and a bow wave of that forest stream cool made his eyes mist and his jaw slacken just a little.

'It will be easy,' she said. 'Literally a pleasure cruise.'

'No one getting hurt?' he checked, his voice drowsy.

'Not if it can be helped. Now—let's go and watch a school hockey match from the sidelines.'

'You're not wearing the boots for it,' he said, before they vanished.

7

Dear Dax

LOL! You're finally getting into Celeb Cellmates! It's brilliant isnt it? Jazmeena SO needs to dump Slap DeFace. Life at schools OK. I'm doing dance now and I'm prob the best one there. Mum bought me four pairs of leather jazz shoes. They are SOOOO kool. LOL.

I'd go on C.C. if I could be famous and get work as a dancer. It would defo be worth it and then, when I was rich, I could just live in a giant manshon with 500 acres and employ a team of gaurds to keep people out if I didn't feel like talking to them. And then when I got married I could have all my pictures in Hello or OK! or something and give the money to charity. Me and Mina both do dance and she says she'll come to stay at the manshon and there'll have to be a river so her dad and brother can come and fish in it. They are bonkers about fishing. I think it's sooooooo boring but Mina says it's good to sit next to a fisher because they give you hedspace.

Their like Zen or something.

So yeah—I'll let them in and when the fame and stuff gets too much and I want to escape I will sit next to Mina's brother (he's fifteen and cute) and let my mind go free. But I won't watch him putting magots on the hooks. That's just disgusting. They explode sometimes.

I havent put chocolate in for Gideon this time because Mum says it'll prob melt in the summer heat.

Got to go. Tiana is coming round to tell me about the latest Dylan drama. She keeps getting back together with him and then breaking up and then getting back . . . she's bonkers. She'll go back to that ex moor than any sane person should! She's a victim.

Byeeeee

Alice

xxx

PS. I am NOT orange. Everyone in the reel world is this colour!

Alice read the letter through and wondered if it was any good. She handed it across the McDonald's table to Caroline.

Caroline scanned it quickly and then glanced up. 'Is your spelling always this bad?'

Alice shrugged. 'Literacy and all that . . . it's not my thing.'

'Good,' Caroline said. 'Then "ex moor" probably won't stand out to them. I just hope they don't pick up on fisher. It's been a long time since my name was on their files. New people have come in . . . hopefully it won't get flagged up as anything suspicious. Well done, Alice.' And she looked at Alice and smiled and nodded as if she was really impressed.

Alice took a deep breath. Caroline Fisher believed they could make a difference. Give Dax an escape route if he needed to take it. It made her feel important. And clever. They had hatched the plan in the cafe and then gone to get some notepaper which looked like the usual stuff Alice used, so she could write the letter and insert the clues. They'd found a table in McDonald's and she'd got on with it while Caroline bought drinks and fries. The journalist kept glancing around. Alice's suspicions about being watched had only been half-serious, she now realized. All the dressing up in disguise with Mina and switching with Tyler had been . . . well, fun. But seeing how seriously this grown woman was taking it all was beginning to affect Alice's nerves. What if the Project intercepted the letter? If Dax picked up the clues hidden in Alice's scrawly handwriting, he would know where to go. But suppose someone else picked up the clues first? Alice shivered and wondered if she should have started all this.

'He might not go there,' said Caroline, thoughtfully tapping the paper. 'It's a place he's been before and the Project would probably go there as soon as he went missing. He'll work that out. BUT . . . he might just scout it out. That's all he needs to do. He won't even need to land to get the message.'

'What will the message be?' asked Alice.

Caroline folded the letter and put it in the stamped envelope. 'Address it,' she said. 'And send it before we leave here. There's a postbox near WHSmith.'

'What's the message?' asked Alice, again.

Caroline touched her hand and smiled. 'Alice—you know they have psychics and telepaths, don't you?'

'Yeah,' said Alice.

'Well . . . I think the least you know about the next bit of the plan, the better,' said Caroline. 'Just in case.'

'But—' Alice looked sulky.

'Seriously. If they do cotton on to something in your letter—they'll come to you first. They might not even need to show up in person to get in to your head.' Alice gulped. She was getting scared. Well, good, thought Caroline. She needed to. 'They can do this kind of thing on the telephone,' she said. 'But they probably *won't* notice anything. Only someone who knows you well would pick it up. And if they *do* try to find out anything, they won't get too far.'

'They'll find out I came to see you!' said Alice, suddenly looking very young and vulnerable.

'Maybe,' said Caroline. 'But they'll still have to catch up with me to find out anything else—and that won't be easy. I'm dropping off the radar for a while.'

'But . . . how will I contact you?' said Alice.

'You won't,' said Caroline, taking out her mobile phone. 'I'll contact you. If there is a need to. But for now . . .' she opened the back of the phone and took out its battery and SIM card ' . . . I will be counting on you to go on being as normal as possible. Just business as usual in Alice World—do you understand?'

Alice nodded. She felt her excitement turning to anxiety as they finished their drinks. Caroline said goodbye and walked away without looking back and Alice wandered across to the postbox. She slid the letter through the slot and held on to its corner for a few seconds. What was she about to do? What would this letter lead to? Maybe nothing. Maybe nothing at all.

She let it drop.

8

The coach was nearly full.

'All aboard the Wifty-Wafty Express,' said Gideon, as he and Dax sat on the steps at the entrance to the lodge. 'Wow. All that lovely healing energy on the motorway. There'll be no road rage today. Everyone will be giving way with a smile and wave and letting caravans pull out, going: "After you! No, really—go right ahead!"'

The Cat. Cs seemed excited and this ought to have made Dax feel better. After all—if something sinister were going on, surely half a coachload of talented psychics would have picked it up from the minds of the COLA Project staff. As well as the inevitable scientists and soldiers, three teachers were off to the spa with them, including Mrs Dann. This should help too, Dax told himself. Mrs Dann had been with the COLAs ever since they had first been discovered, five years ago. He trusted her. She wouldn't get involved with anything which wasn't totally up front.

'Stop worrying, Fox Boy.' Lisa had arrived on the step behind. He got up and turned to her.

'I can't help it,' he said. 'I—I just—'

'It'll be fine,' said Lisa. 'Sylv would be doing her nut if she thought I was in any danger. All she's picking up is extreme relaxation. Like it or not.' She cast her eyes heavenward.

Sylv was Lisa's spirit guide—and as blunt and fearless as Lisa when it came to frank conversations. She looked out for her teenage medium and helped keep the incessant flow of dead people away from Lisa when she needed a break.

'Well, if Sylv says it's OK . . .' Dax knotted his fingers in his hair and let out a long breath. He wanted to stop Lisa going. Right now. He wanted to grab her hand and run. The feeling was so strong he had to gulp it down and take a long deep breath.

Lisa put her expensive suede bag down at her feet. She reached up, put her hands on the angles of his cheekbones and tilted her head, watching him closely. 'I would go with you,' she said, softly. 'But what makes you think I'm any safer in here than out there?'

Dax opened his mouth to speak but she rested one finger across it, bridging his upper and lower lip. 'You're not worried about me, Dax,' she said, a smile touching her face for the first time in days. 'You've just realized you're going to miss me.'

Dax closed his eyes for a moment as an intense scent flowed over him. It came from Lisa and what it told him was unmistakable. Shocking.

She kissed him before he could even exhale and that was more shocking still. Warm and sweet; familiar and yet wildly unfamiliar. He was dimly aware of Gideon saying 'Wow. I mean . . . Wow . . .' but then the voice was lost below him and Lisa was getting onto the coach with her bag and he was high, high above.

Well, what else would he do but fly?

She was right. He *was* going to miss her. Badly. The realization was a hot ache inside him. He flew along the winding drive, coasting just above the coach. At the tinted rear window, Lisa leant a slender arm along the back of the seat and gazed up at him.

As they reached the perimeter the electronic gates slowly opened and the dark thrum of the magnetic field pushed him back.

The last words he heard from Lisa's mind were, *I'll miss you too, Dax. I really will.*

Dax landed back beside Gideon a minute later and shifted back to boy form.

'Well. That was unexpected,' said Gideon. He was grinning at Dax and he reached out and prodded his friend's shoulder. 'You sly fox!'

Dax turned to stare at him and Gideon let out a laugh, shaking his head. 'Mate—you should see your face!'

Dax dragged a tangled sentence out of his recently scrambled brain. The words had to duck and dive past wave after wave of unfamiliar emotion. 'I—what? I mean . . . Lees . . . I will miss . . . she said she'd . . . what?'

Gideon gave him a hug and then a punch on the shoulder. He was laughing so hard there were tears in his eyes. 'You are SO stupid you don't even know it!' he burbled. 'Did you not know? How could you not know? You and Lisa? EVERYONE knows it. Everyone has known it for YEARS.'

* * *

The coach was filled with chattering girls and a handful of quieter boys. Lisa arranged herself on the back seat in a way which discouraged anyone from joining her. She sat with her shoulders against the window and rested her legs, in their pale lemon designer jeans and golden suede sandals, along the seat, taking up at least three spaces. Just beyond her polished toes lay her Fendi gold suede bag, filled with her personal stuff. The bag alone probably cost more than everything else the rest of the COLAs on this coach were wearing.

Only one other COLA had dared get close to where she was sitting—a girl with long dark hair and hazel eyes, who had taken the window on the far side, edging past Lisa's bag and making no attempt to encroach on her space.

Lisa needed to be left alone. She got enough chatter from dead people, let alone living ones. And she needed to try to work out why she had just kissed Dax Jones. Why now? It wasn't that she hadn't thought about it for some time; she had. Truth was, the idea of a kiss with COLA Club's only shapeshifter had flitted through her mind more than once over the past three years. She'd resisted it. Romance in a school? Doomed. No way was she going there. What if it all fell horribly apart? You couldn't escape. In an ordinary school you'd be dealing with it five days a week, ducking away from your ex and trying to pretend he didn't exist. But at Fenton Lodge? You were cooped up with everyone day and night! The place was seething with gossip. With so little information from the outside world allowed in, COLA Club made its own entertainment. And Lisa was being talked about quite enough already. Nobody there liked her, apart from Dax, Gideon, and Luke. Well . . . the Teller brothers—Jacob and Alex—they thought she was OK. Maybe Barry and Jennifer . . .

A rumour had come out recently that most of the scientists at COLA Club believed the students might already have peaked. If it was true none of the duds ever would catch up with Lisa, that was a whole bucketload of resentment. It buzzed and whined in their heads whenever they encountered her. Any time she liked, Lisa could slip into their minds like a knife through butter and find out the detail . . .

. . . *stuck up cow walks around like she owns the place so impressed with herself like she's better than all of us and yeah she looks great but she's always got such a sour look on her perfect little face hasn't she and they say her best friend tried to set fire to her before she left and I wouldn't blame her would you because she's so smug with all her rich bitch clothes and bags and shoes and oh yeah there's a pony back at home isn't there daddy's little princess and why can't I get in her head I'm psychic too I should be able to get something from her head and oh God she's in my head she's in here get out you're in here how come you can get in when I've got my shutters down BECAUSE YOU'RE AN IDIOT AND YOU DON'T KNOW WHAT THE HELL YOU'RE DOING, THAT'S WHY. NICE TRY, THOUGH.*

And that's pretty much where the conversation ended, before either party had even opened their mouths. Lisa had learned foolproof shuttering techniques even before her first year in COLA Club was up. She had a mind gate worthy of the Bank of England vaults. The look on their shocked little faces almost made her laugh out loud. Dax was always telling her to ease off and stop messing with them . . . and she would, except they occasionally needed putting in their place, little dud upstarts.

Dax. Ah yes. Back to Dax. The kiss. Why now? Just because she was going away for a few days? It was all the panic she'd picked up in his head . . . that thing about wanting to grab her hand and run away into the trees. It had been so . . . no . . . not sweet. That was not the word. True, maybe. Something pure and true and sweet but not sugary. Nothing about Dax was sugary.

Maybe it was because she knew she'd miss him too. As simple as that. So she'd done a thing that millions of teenage girls all around the world were doing every day. She'd kissed a boy. That's all. *Oh yeah?* said Sylv, suddenly close by in her head. She gave a throaty cackle. *You keep telling yourself that, love. Whatever.*

'Do you want a mint?'

Lisa jumped at this voice from the real world. The dark-haired girl was holding out a roll of Polos. She smiled sympathetically. 'You looked like you might be getting a bit coach-sick! I get that way too sometimes. I have to sit by a window and look out and eat mints.'

Lisa instinctively scanned the girl's thoughts for the usual resentment and jealousy but found none. Sure, there was a gate—a better than average one—but what she could glimpse through it without even trying was calm . . . pale blue.

'No?' the girl said, with a little shrug. 'Well, let me know if you change your mind.'

'I will,' said Lisa. 'Thanks.' She sat up and angled herself so she could look out of the window too, as the Cumbrian countryside blurred past.

'Love the bag, by the way,' went on the girl. 'Fendi, isn't it?'

Lisa sighed and turned back to her. 'Yes. Well spotted. Look—I don't mean to be nasty but I'm just not very chatty right now, OK?'

The girl laughed—but not in a mean way. 'I know,' she said. 'You kind of never are.'

Lisa opened her mouth to say something waspish—to shut this conversation down once and for all—but the girl was smiling at her almost as if she was waiting for exactly that. And the laughter in her voice was sparking across her eyes. Lisa screwed up her face and shook her head. Of course. This one wasn't a psychic. She was a healer. A good one. Probably the best of all the duds because she was the first to make any impression at all on Lisa. She wasn't at Mia's level, of course . . .

The girl spoke again. 'My name's—'

'Tilly,' cut in Lisa. 'You're a healer. You're from Ipswich and you have a baby half-sister called Lucy and a dog called Wuffles—*seriously*?!—and you get eczema and it gets bad when you're stressed out by doing too much healing because you haven't properly learned how to protect yourself yet but you're still better than most of the others and you wanted to be a singer before you got kidnapped by COLA Club—twice—but you're making the best of it and now you just want to be the best healer in the world. Big surprise.'

Tilly was quiet for a few beats. Then she just said 'Ouch.'

Lisa shrugged. 'Your gate's not locked.'

'Sure—come on in—help yourself.'

'I'm done,' said Lisa, turning back to the window. But actually, she wasn't. She had found something else in Tilly's mind. She should have ignored it but she realized she couldn't.

After nearly a minute she gave up the fight and turned back to her coach-mate. 'Look—Tilly—tell me something.'

'What? You mean you can't just mind read your answer?' The words were sharp but the girl was actually laughing again. A bit like the way Mia had laughed at her, refusing to take her snippiness seriously until she stopped snipping and niced up.

Lisa took a deep breath and then went on in a low voice. 'How long have they been asking you to make a flame?'

Tilly blinked. 'What . . . in Development? Umm . . . a few weeks. They'll probably give up soon; I'm useless at it. Everyone is.'

'So . . . nobody's done it yet?'

'No—I keep trying, when I'm on my own mostly; it's

easier to concentrate without people spying on you the whole time. But no. My hands get quite hot when I'm healing but not, like, *spontaneous combustion* hot!'

Lisa let out a sigh. 'Dear God, can you all be so stupid?'

The girl looked at her, seriously. 'Lisa—you're not winning any friends with this stuff. We all know you think we're stupid. Duds.'

Lisa shook her head. 'Stop trying,' she said. 'For God's sake. You seem like you might have half a brain cell. Try to work it out. What will happen if you make fire for them? What do you *think* will happen? A gold certificate and a badge? An iced cake? Cat. A status? What do you think that *means?!*'

Tilly said nothing. She sat back and ate another Polo. At length she muttered 'Better off a dud, eh?'

'Believe it,' said Lisa, putting in some earbuds and switching on her iPod. She angled back to the window and the girl did not bother her again.

9

Caroline Fisher bumped her old Toyota 4 x 4 around the narrow lanes of North Devon. She wished she could relax a little: her shoulders were like knotted piano wire. Two or three times on her journey along the M4, heading out of London, she had thought a car was following her. But on each occasion she had dawdled in the inside lane until the driver had overtaken. She had not noticed anything else for the past hour.

Anyway, it had been years since she'd been a person of interest to the COLA Project. And even then, all she had done was allow Dax and his friends to stay in her cottage—The Owl Box—for a couple of days. She hadn't even been there herself; Dax had a key—something she'd given him way back, shortly after he'd saved her life; a place to escape to should he ever need it. A thank you— and an apology for all the stress she'd caused him by tracking him down and trying to expose his secret in the press. She had been a very much younger reporter back then—in many ways.

Dax still had that key as far as she knew and she had never changed the locks. Even so, she didn't think he would go there in a crisis again—not without expecting to be followed hours later; the COLA Project knew about it. They'd chased him and his friends out of it last time. It was too obvious a place to run to.

No—the only way he would come to Exmoor again was if he picked up the clues in Alice's letter. 'Fisher' and 'ex moor'—Caroline's surname and the location of The Owl Box. Today was the earliest the letter could have reached him. Who knew how long it took to get past all the COLA Project checks? And even then . . . was Dax *really* intending to escape and leave his friends behind? Maybe not. She shivered. She might be putting herself to a lot of trouble for a bit of teenage angst which wouldn't lead to anything. But if he really did need to get away, she wanted to help. And if nothing else, her plan would give her a little thinking time about her own future. She could bear to watch the sea and ponder for a few days.

Caroline turned a sharp left and the Toyota began to descend the rough, overgrown driveway to the cottage. It was high time she came down here and did a bit of maintenance. She hadn't been here since her two-week break at Christmas and New Year. She should clear corners of cobwebs and country spiders, check the chimney for bird nests, bring in some logs, and fire up the woodburner. Some other time she would. Today she only needed to climb up and check the thatch on the roof. With some pins.

That was the most important thing.

The plastic-covered note in her pocket was brief and to the point. It would be meaningless to virtually everyone except Dax and herself. After a quick cup of coffee in the cottage, Caroline took a deep breath and went to fetch the ladder. She did not enjoy heights. It occurred to her that this might be a total waste of time. Dax would probably never come here.

Even so, she knew she had to do this. Just in case. COLA allies were few and far between and she was still one of them, whoever else had forgotten it.

Twenty minutes later she was sitting astride the thatched ridge of the cottage, trying not to panic. The roof was a lot higher than it looked from the ground. Although the trees clustered closely around, she was neurotic about drones or even satellite spy cameras. *Seriously? Get a grip, Fisher!* she told herself. *You're not that interesting.* She pressed the paper, wrapped in plastic, to the side of the ridge which wasn't viewable from the road approach. Then she pinned it in place. Another twenty minutes passed before the Toyota bumped back up the driveway to the narrow lane. The cottage was locked up securely and probably nobody would ever know she'd been there. At the T-junction with the B road she checked around her. Nobody in sight on the road or anywhere near it. With a shiver she turned south.

10

The brothers in Cat. A couldn't argue that they had been misplaced.

Gideon and Luke's telekinetic powers were so strong it was rumoured that flight paths across Cumbria had been adjusted so no plane ever crossed the skies above the Fenton Lodge estate. Just in case one of the Reader twins rerouted it for a laugh with a hard stare. Nobody was sure this rumour was true—after all, Luke and Gideon had done some amazingly helpful things for the government with their ability and they had never attempted anything harmful. They were good and decent people; all the psychiatric tests confirmed this. But times changed. Governments changed. People got scared. And it was a very long time since Dax had seen a vapour trail.

Luke looked a lot like Gideon; they were genetically identical. Luke wore glasses, though, and chose to dye his hair almost black. He'd experimented with the dye last year and stuck with it. It suited him and both brothers liked to be different in appearance. They were very different in character too. For a start, Gideon was always on the go and rarely shut up, while Luke liked to read in quiet corners and barely spoke at all.

His ability to speak had been taken from him some years ago and although he was beginning to recover, he still tended to remain quiet. Speaking took effort and concentration. He and Gideon found it easier to lapse back into sign language most of the time. They had been separated while they were still babies and hadn't even met until they were thirteen—but they loved each other.

And they loved their dad.

Maybe they would have known about it sooner if all the psychics hadn't been bussed off to a spa holiday, but the next morning found Gideon and Luke Reader in a state of shock and horror.

At breakfast they got a note to see Forrester. When they returned to the lodge they were ashen-faced, with twin expressions of dismay.

'What's happened?' said Dax, as soon as he found them in the dorm he and Gideon shared.

Luke glanced across and shook his head. Distress usually rendered him mute again.

'It's Dad,' said Gideon. His voice was thick; close to choking. Dax felt the hairs rise on his neck and arms. 'He was hit by a truck,' Gideon went on. He shoved more clothes into a small holdall and took a long breath. His eyes were red-rimmed.

'What? Will he . . . ?'

'We don't know. He's alive but he's hurt and we don't know if he'll make it. He's in intensive care. They're flying us down now.' Gideon gulped and looked at Dax. 'They're letting us *out*, Dax. What does that tell you?'

Dax gave his best friend a hug. He didn't know what else to do. Gideon took the hug for a few seconds and then resumed his packing. Luke stood still, his bag already filled, waiting for his brother. Behind his glasses his green eyes were downcast. The brothers might like to look different but today fear and sorrow haunted their faces in precisely the same pattern. Dax hugged Luke too and felt him shaking.

Dax followed them out to the waiting helicopter and stood back, out of the downdraft, as they climbed aboard with Forrester. The man's thin face wore an expression of care and sympathy. Dax wished it could be a little more convincing. He wished he didn't scent such alienation in Forrester. He wished—oh how he wished— that David Chambers had never gone away and this man had not been brought in to run the COLA Project in his place. The whole thing stank. If Chambers *had* just been promoted, why hadn't he come back to tell them all himself? He had *cared* about them; Dax knew it.

It brought home to him how little control he or any of the other COLAs had over their world. If the man they trusted to run their college—their *lives*—could be removed without warning, what else might happen at the whim of the government? This was no private mansion run by Dr Xavier in the X-Men. As much as their families joked about it, COLA life was not like a Marvel comic. It wasn't glossy. It was real. Their world was funded by the government. The COLA Project was actually part of the Ministry of Defence. Decisions about their future lay with politicians, civil servants, and the military. Certainly not with themselves.

The chopper was lifting off now. Gideon and Luke sat within the Perspex bubble, too downcast to wave at him as they rose above the grounds. Forrester waved, though. He smiled too. It chilled Dax to see it.

A hand rested on his shoulder. The downdraft from the helicopter had blown the scent away but he instantly knew it was Mr Tucker, one of the teachers.

'Are you OK, Dax?' Dax turned to the tall, lanky, grey-haired man as the helicopter disappeared on the horizon. He smiled weakly back at him and shrugged.

'Tough times,' Mr Tucker said. 'I really hope Mr Reader will pull through. I think they're getting a couple of the better healers to leave the spa and meet them at the hospital, but . . .'

He didn't need to go on. They both knew that none of the other healers were on the scale of Mia. They could do amazing things but it took time. Sharing a room with a COLA healer for a few hours would speed up your recovery time by double or even more. But nobody could mend a broken bone with a touch—not like Mia.

'Well,' concluded Mr Tucker, 'maybe Tilly will go. She's very promising. Getting better every day in Development. Which I'm told, is where you're wanted now, Dax.'

Mr Tucker walked back to the lodge with him. 'I won't see you for a while, either,' he said. 'I'm off for a little watercolour break in the south of France.'

'Well—have a good time,' Dax said as they crossed the lodge hallway. He stifled a sigh. Lisa was gone. Gideon and Luke were gone. Now his other favourite teacher was heading off.

'Don't look so worried!' Mr Tucker said. 'We'll all be back before you know it. I'll bring you something from St. Tropez.' His face creased with concern. 'Dax—I know everything's been strange since David Chambers went but it will settle down. Don't worry.'

Dax lifted his chin and gave his teacher the sort of optimistic smile he knew he was hoping for.

'And hey! We'll have your GCSE results when I get back, won't we?'

Dax rolled his eyes. 'Yeah—thanks for that!'

Mr Tucker gave him a half-hug, in an unteachery way, and then left him to head down to the Development rooms alone.

The basement level was where all Development took place. Subterranean rooms cocooned in blast-proof concrete were where COLAs were routinely tested and scrutinized by the scientists. Dax didn't attend many Development sessions these days, just a once a week calibration or psych test. There wasn't much to him, after all. His talent was very cut and dried. He could change shape at will—into three alternative animal forms. The scientists liked to look at his brain when he was in animal form but even with all the new security pushes, they knew they could only do that so many times before it got a. medically dangerous and b. a bit dull. They were hoping,

Dax sensed, that he might change into something else one day. Just to liven things up a bit.

Today's session was with Ros, a psychiatrist and counsellor. It was her job to report back on his state of mind at regular intervals. Dax quite liked her but he was anxious not to let her know how worried he was. Since Forrester and all his bright new security ideas had arrived, Dax did not want to share his thoughts and feelings with anyone who worked for the COLA Project. They all had an agenda. A job to keep. A manager to report to. With the possible exception of Mrs Dann and Mr Tucker, he did not trust anybody here on the staff.

'Hi Dax,' said Ros, a willowy woman in her forties, with wavy dark hair and a thing for purple. 'Don't freak out on me, but today you'll need to strip down to your undies.'

Dax blinked. 'Erm . . . why?'

She smiled and waved over a younger woman, in a white tunic. 'This is Corinne. She's an aromatherapist.'

Corinne looked serene and professional. Her long fair hair was in a side plait and she smiled through a light touch of lip gloss. The brown leather case she was carrying was almost overwhelming his nostrils. It was full of essential oils.

'Look, I'm not really in the mood for a massage.'

'Nobody needs a massage more,' said Corinne, with a light southern Irish accent, 'than when they're not in the mood for one.'

Dax sighed. 'Really?' he asked Ros.

She nodded. 'We want to see what effect it has on your body chemistry. It's very low key, though. Nothing to worry about.'

'It doesn't smell very low key,' muttered Dax, pulling his T-shirt off.

He had to admit, though, that Corinne was good. He lay on his front and she worked the pungent oils into his skin in a rhythmic massage across his back and shoulders. 'There's a lot of tension here,' she murmured. He didn't answer. The massage and the intense bittersweet perfume (bergamot, lavender, and thyme, Corinne told him) was relaxing and making him sleepy.

Really sleepy.

So sleepy, in fact, that . . .

11

Dax bolted upright as if he'd been fired from a cannon. He was in his bed, across from Gideon's, which was still crumpled from packing up and leaving that morning. Only . . . what?! The light wasn't mid-afternoon or even late-afternoon light. It was *morning* light. The clock beside him read 9.17 a.m.

How had he got here? Where had the last eighteen hours gone? Who had dressed him in pyjamas?

And why was everything so quiet?

In an instant he was out of the window and circling the house. He wasn't flying well. His head was foggy and his navigation was off. His wing clipped a tree branch. But a swift circle around the house showed that nobody was about. He flew back to his room, shifted to boy, and ran out into the corridor. He stood still. Nothing. He shifted to fox to listen. There was nobody on this floor. Nobody. Maybe everyone was downstairs at breakfast? It wasn't term time now and whatever activities were planned tended to start around mid-morning. Most of the COLAs dragged themselves down to breakfast about twenty minutes before they needed to be somewhere. It was 9.25 now. They *could* all be downstairs.

Only they weren't. He could smell and hear that they

weren't. He ran down to check in any case. The dining hall was empty; its shutters pulled down across the serving area. Nothing was being cooked behind them. The common room was also eerily silent. But there were people about. He could smell them—distantly. He followed his nose and was guided to the corridor where most of the Cat. Bs now had dorms.

And here he uncovered what was left of COLA Club. Pushing open a door he found Jacob and Alex Teller asleep. They were in pyjamas and bundled up in quilts despite the warmth of the day. Asleep. But not in the normal way. He could smell something odd on them; a bitter scent which seemed vaguely familiar.

And he realized now where he'd smelled it before. It had been masked by bergamot, lavender, and thyme—but yes, it had been there, mixed into the essential oils that Corinne had massaged into his back eighteen hours ago.

He had been drugged. And so had they.

Dax shifted back to boy form and began to shake Alex awake. The boy groaned and stared up at him blearily. 'Alex! How long have you been asleep?!' he demanded.

Alex sat up, shoving the bedding off him. 'What? What's the matter?'

'When did you go to bed?'

'Um . . . I don't know . . .' Alex wiped his hand across his brown fringe and screwed his face up. 'Why?'

But Dax was shaking Jacob awake now.

Jacob groaned, sat up, and then shook his head vigorously. 'I feel weird,' he said. 'What's going on?'

'Did you get the aromatherapy massage?' demanded Dax. 'Did everyone?'

They nodded. 'She was hot,' mumbled Jacob. 'That Irish girl.'

'Yeah. And she was drugging you,' stated Dax. 'There was something in the massage oil. They know they can't tamper with our food, so they got around it by drugging us through the skin.'

They looked appalled. 'Why?

'I think I know. Wait here a minute.' Dax shifted to fox, stepped outside their room, and inhaled deeply. He listened for a few seconds and then sprinted up and down the corridor, checking out what his senses told him. When he returned to Jacob and Alex five minutes later, he had confirmed it.

'All the Cat. As are gone,' he said. 'All of them. It's just Cat. Bs left here now. Seventeen Cat. As disappeared *overnight*—and all the Cat. Bs just slept through it.'

The Teller brothers threw their clothes on and accompanied Dax around the lodge, knocking on doors and peering into dorms. Everyone was still in bed. Everyone had had the aromatherapy massage. After ten minutes Dax went to get properly dressed and the three regrouped in the dining room, where noises behind the metal shutters of the serving area revealed the catering staff were now in.

Dax knocked hard on the shutters and a few seconds later Mrs P., looking a little perplexed in her tunic and tabard, appeared. 'What's the panic?' she asked, scanning the three of them.

'Where have you been?' demanded Dax. 'Why weren't you in earlier?'

She wrinkled her brow beneath strands of grey hair that escaped her cotton cap. 'We had a late start today. We were told—no breakfast—just brunch. We had a works do last night!' She giggled. 'Yes! We *do* have a life, you know! Mr Forrester organized a dinner and a disco, would you believe?! We left cold stuff for your breakfast yesterday before we all went off. Didn't you find it?'

Dax, Jacob, and Alex stared at each other. Eventually Dax muttered, 'Sorry . . . we forgot.'

'Come back in twenty minutes!' said Mrs P., smiling at them indulgently. 'I can have some bacon butties ready for you.'

'Thanks . . . but . . . don't worry,' said Dax and they left the dining room. They walked through the hall and out onto the wide step outside the imposing front door of the lodge where they sat in silence for a few seconds.

'So,' said Alex, at length. 'They want to take the Cat. Cs away, so they set up this spa break thing. Job done. And then they want to take the Cat. As away. Why not just give them a holiday too?'

'All of them together?' said Jacob. 'The security would have to be mammoth for that many Cat. As. I mean, most of them aren't that scary, but Luke and Gideon—'

'Luke and Gideon left yesterday morning, remember?' cut in Dax. 'They got them out of the way first, in the helicopter. I wonder if their dad really was in an accident at all. I think Forrester just wanted to remove them before coming for all the others. He didn't want trouble.'

'So . . .' Jacob went on. 'They take Gid and Luke away and then the rest of the Cat. As . . . and now we're the only ones left. The Cat. Bs. What the hell is going on?'

'Ask him,' said Dax, flicking his thumb back over his shoulder. He did not need to look to know that Forrester was standing in the doorway, just behind them. He could smell the man clearly. It made his nostrils flare with disgust.

'I'm happy to explain,' said Forrester. 'Why don't you all come to my office?'

They walked in silence across the grounds to the modern wing which housed David Chambers's office; now Forrester's. He hadn't changed much inside the room; the leather couch was the same; the desk was the same—it just held different files and a new laptop. A tall arched window gave on to a view of cedars. It had always been a calming place, thought Dax; he had liked the smell of it. Not any more.

Forrester sat in the leather chair on the far side of the desk and nodded towards the couch. 'Take a seat,' he said, and they all sat down and stared at him.

'First let me assure you, nobody else is going anywhere. All Category B students will now remain at Fenton Lodge.'

Dax and the Teller brothers exchanged looks. 'Are we meant to feel better?' asked Dax.

Forrester gave him that thin smile again. 'I doubt

anything I can say to *you* will make you feel better, Dax but I hope Jacob and Alex will find it comforting that they are not to be uprooted.'

'What's happened to everyone else?' demanded Dax. 'Where have you taken them?'

Forrester thumbed a button on his desk and his intercom buzzed through to the secretary who had once served Chambers. 'Hector—coffee,' he said. Dax didn't think it was for all of them. The man sat back in his chair and smiled again. 'What you have to understand is the bigger picture,' he said. 'A new Prime Minister arrives in office and the old one leaves—taking with him many experiences, ideas, values ... Our ex-PM was rather soft where the COLA Project was concerned; David Chambers ran rings around him.'

Dax compressed his lips; he had met the ex-PM and was certain nobody could run even half a ring around the man.

'Of course, you and Miss Hardman saved the PM's life last year, which surely would have helped him to think well of you both,' said Forrester. 'He allowed Chambers to give you all far too much slack. And look what happened—one deranged COLA tried to burn your college to the ground. And now she and her accomplice are missing and probably plotting more destruction. This is the kind of thing we really cannot allow. All three of you were involved in what happened last year so I need hardly remind you of how close we all came to annihilation.'

'We?' said Dax, coldly. 'I don't think you were there.'

Forrester ignored him. 'Security was lax and far too much freedom was given to you all. We cherish our COLAs—but we must protect them from the world. And we must protect the *world* from our COLAs. I'm sure you understand.'

They said nothing. Forrester wasn't asking for feedback.

'So it was decided that the safest way to nurture your talents was by categorizing you all in terms of what you could offer to your country . . . and what threat you might pose to it. Once we had streamed you all into appropriate categories, it was obvious that housing Children of Limitless Ability *together* was a dangerous policy. Let's be practical. Just one hit from a renegade COLA like Mia Cooper, and every member of COLA Club could be a smoking pile of charcoal.'

'Mia would never do that!' snapped Dax. He felt his fingernails dig into the leather of the couch.

'As I recall,' said Forrester, arching one eyebrow. '*You* were one of her victims last year. Lucky not to end up as spit roast.'

'She was being manipulated by Spook Williams— you know that! Or don't you read the files?'

'Thoroughly,' replied Forrester. 'That's why we're having this conversation. Spook is also a major threat to you. So . . . to continue—we've been building new sites— as well as fortifying this one—and now we have separated you into three groups. Dax—you are the reason that the Cat. Bs have remained here at Fenton Lodge. You alone require a large area to fly in; therefore we decided to keep you here. And your fellow Cat. Bs get to stay here along with you. Cat. As are potentially the most dangerous—so they are now housed in a suitable compound, elsewhere in the UK. A safe place where they can't get into trouble. It was necessary to remove Gideon and Luke first—with a certain regrettable subterfuge.'

'Their dad's *not* hurt?' asked Alex. 'You faked it?'

The man nodded and Dax, remembering the horror on his best friend's face twenty-four hours ago, felt rage boiling through his chest.

'They were told as soon as it was safe; once they had reached their new home,' Forrester said. 'And the Cat. Cs, as you know, are in a beautiful retreat elsewhere in the country. We told them it was a break—and it is. It's just that the break is *permanent*.'

'So . . . that's it?' said Jacob. 'You take our friends away and you tell us *nothing*?'

'It would not have helped anyone to know,' said Forrester. 'You would all have been very upset.'

'Bloody right we would!' said Jacob. He shook his head. 'How come Lisa and all the psychics didn't see this coming?' he murmured. 'How come *we* didn't?' He glanced at his brother. 'We should have picked this up!'

'You couldn't,' said Forrester. 'Not even with telepathy. Nobody here knew of the plan. Not a single person. Just me . . . and the Prime Minister. The contractors we have employed have been working without any additional information; they have no clue what they have been building or why. Our science team and your teachers knew nothing of this; we strategically arranged for most employee holidays to occur at this point. I needed only a small crew, brought up from London, to execute the plan. The boarding and catering staff were removed while the rest of the Cat. As were collected last night. There was no struggle among those students; no distress—*they* had massages too.' He grinned and something gleeful sparked across his small eyes. 'And don't be too hard on Ros and Corinne. They only knew they were trying out some new 'relaxation methods' for the Cat Cs. And they were only told *after* we'd removed all those mind readers to a safe distance. There is nobody here for you to rail at, Dax,' he glanced over as Dax gritted his teeth and scored the leather more deeply. 'Nobody but me.' He smiled again. 'And we're both used to that, aren't we?'

'You'll never keep Gideon and Luke in!' said Jacob. 'Wherever you've put them. They can break open a mountain!'

'I think not,' said Forrester. 'And in any case . . . we have measures in place. Now—if you don't mind, I have work to do. Try not to be too upset. This really is what's best for everyone.'

It was all Dax could do not to shift and rip the man's throat out. He closed his eyes.

Alex was grabbing his arm. 'Come on, Dax,' he said. 'Let's go.'

As they left the office, Dax glanced at Hector, the thin young man who had been Chambers's devoted secretary for three years. As the office door closed behind them, Dax said: 'Did you know? Did you know what he was going to do?'

Hector stared at Dax. He had always been scared of the COLAs. But underneath the pungency of fear, Dax could smell his sorrow. Hector had *loved* Chambers. The young man adjusted his tie and shook his head. 'I have to take coffee in,' he said. The cup rattled in the saucer as he carried it past them. 'Just go.'

There was a special assembly later in the day, where Forrester addressed all the remaining students and told them what he'd told Dax, Alex, and Jacob. He put it differently; more gently—but by then everyone had heard about it from Jacob and Alex and they were appalled and angry. No teachers accompanied them in the large school hall but a soldier stood to attention in every corner. None were actually holding rifles but the message was clear. *No trouble.* There were shouts and questions anyway, and some of the girls were crying openly, realizing they would not be seeing friends again.

'I urge you all to relax,' said Forrester. 'This situation cannot be reversed. It's for the best. So . . . accept it. Have a lovely summer—we have lots of fun events lined up for you and visiting family—and by the time your new term starts you will all have got used to this. You'll build new friendships and face new challenges together and above all—you'll be safe.'

Dax found himself staring at Clive. Clive stood in the middle of the students, next to Barry. Clive was lucky. He had not lost his best friend—or his second best. For a moment his gaze shifted across to Dax, whose friendship had brought him here, and he looked deeply troubled. His place in all this was confusing. For Clive wasn't a Cat. B. Or a Cat. C or a Cat. A. Clive had no category among the COLAs at all, because he wasn't one.

As everyone walked out past the soldiers and spread into the sunshine outside, some in stunned silence, others talking agitatedly or crying, Clive made his way across to Dax and fixed him with wide dark-grey eyes, framed by spectacles. 'What are you going to do, Dax?' he whispered, although nobody was anywhere near them.

'What makes you think I'm going to do anything at all?' muttered Dax.

'Maybe it's because I've known you since you were six . . . ?'

Dax nodded and gave his old friend a wan smile. 'You have, too,' he said. They walked on towards the woods, taking their own path away from the others.

Clive was the only friend Dax still had from his old, pre-COLA life. Clive shouldn't be here at COLA Club at all—and he certainly never would have been if Forrester had been in charge from the start instead of Chambers. But what Clive lacked in COLA powers he made up for in pure brilliance. He was a genius. When Dax, Lisa, Gideon, and Mia had been on the run together, hiding out in Caroline Fisher's cottage, Clive had tracked them and found them—and then saved their skins with his quirky, awkward cleverness.

But then, Dax had saved *Clive's* skin a year before, when they were still at junior school and he had first begun to shapeshift. He had fought off Clive's attackers . . . and accidentally allowed Clive to see him change from boy to fox. This was the chief reason Clive had later been allowed to join Dax at Fenton Lodge. After the boy had got caught up in the COLA adventures on Exmoor, David Chambers had decided that it was safer to have Clive on the inside. He also thought he'd be useful to the scientists who were studying the COLAs. They could use his non-COLA brain as a comparison to the others when they did their various tests.

Clive had loved it. He never looked back. He'd arrived, a short, bespectacled, skinny boy with terrible fashion sense and poor social skills. Now he was a tall, bespectacled, skinny teenager . . . with terrible fashion sense and slightly improved social skills. He already had eight A* grade A Levels under his belt and was halfway through a science degree. He regularly helped out with the scientists assigned to the COLA Project and was certain his career lay right here, alongside all the COLAs. Part of the Project. He was devoted.

Only . . . how did he feel *now?* Where did he put himself when his friends were being treated this way?

'Did you know . . . anything?' Dax asked.

Clive looked stung. 'Of *course* not! What do you take me for?'

Dax felt bad immediately. He gripped Clive's shoulder. 'I'm sorry . . . I know. I just don't know what to think about anyone any more. And the scientists . . . the people you do your work with , . . what are they saying?'

'Most of them are away,' said Clive. 'Only a few are still here; the ones who care more about the science than the students,' he admitted. 'Believe it or not, a lot of them care about you guys as much as I do. Well, maybe not *that* much, but close. None of them knew the gameplan, I promise you. I would have heard something.'

'But they must have suspected something—with all the extra security and wall building and . . .' he paused. 'Clive . . . did they tell you about the dome?'

Clive looked stunned. He went pink and glanced away from Dax, biting his lips together for a moment. 'They . . . they've really done it?' he asked, at length. 'They made a dome?'

Dax nodded. 'You knew?'

He shook his head. 'Not for certain. Not until now. Why didn't you tell me?'

'Why didn't you tell *me*?'

Clive blinked and shook his head. 'I really didn't think they'd do it. I didn't think it was *possible* to make a defined dome from an EM field.'

'Well, they did,' said Dax. 'But I haven't told anyone. Forrester—he made threats. Gideon knew about the steel walls and the underground barriers; the gates across the waterways—anyone who had eyes knew about those. But if I'd told him about the dome I think he might have lost it . . . done something. And got himself into really bad trouble.'

'Can the dome really keep you in?' breathed Clive.

'Yes,' said Dax. 'So you *did* know *something*, Clive.'

'No—I mean—nobody told me,' said Clive. 'I overheard.' He stopped near the tree house Dax and Gideon had spent ages building a few summers back, glancing up uneasily. 'Is anyone up there?'

'No,' said Dax. He could smell nobody up in the branches.

'Alright—look, I was working with one of the lab teams and I'd finished up and gone home but I remembered something I needed in one of the supply cupboards and nipped back in for it. The door was sort of half-closed behind me and I heard Doctor LeGuin and his assistant talking. I wasn't even aware that I was listening; I was hunting through the shelves for some phials . . . but anyway, I heard them talk about *you*. About the "Dax Jones Problem". And that's when I started listening properly.'

'And you heard about the dome?'

'No—not exactly. They were talking in fluent science, OK? I could reel off all the maths to you but you wouldn't understand. I only heard some of it. They never knew I was in there, listening. They know you're my friend— they'd never talk about the Dax Jones Problem in front of me.'

'But you still didn't say anything to me?' Dax said, getting impatient.

'No—because—I didn't know what it meant! It was only later that I worked out what the formula was *for*. An electromagnetic force field. But—Dax—I thought it was *impossible*! Nobody has ever been able to focus an electromagnetic field that tightly. Not even in MRI scanners—that's why you can't take a watch or a phone into the room. That much energy can't be contained in a narrow, defined shape; it floods out into everything. If there's a huge dome over us, every electrical thing in this place should be going haywire! It's not possible!'

'Well, trust me, they've found a way,' snapped Dax. He rounded on Clive. 'You should have warned me! If I had known what was coming I could have got away before they put it in place!'

'But . . . but you wouldn't have,' said Clive, his voice falling to a whisper. There were tears welling up in his eyes. 'You'd never have left Lisa and Gideon, would you?'

Dax closed his eyes and tried to beat down the wave of devastation he felt when he realized Gideon and Lisa might never be in his life again. He pressed his palms to his face and took a deep breath.

'I'm sorry,' said Clive. 'I *should* have told you. I was just so sure they'd never pull it off.'

'They pulled it off, all right,' said Dax. 'They even got me to test it for them.' And he related the day when he'd been brought out of Development, up to a remote meadow, and made to fly through the electromagnetic field.

Clive sat down beneath the trees. 'Describe it to me again,' he said. 'Tell me exactly what it looked like—the two rigs.'

Dax described them.

Clive got to his feet and Dax saw a brainstorm flickering across his friend's eyes. 'Dax . . . I know where they keep those. I've seen them,' he said.

'OK,' said Dax. 'Well . . . what?'

'You can try the field out again,' said Clive.

'What—for the fun of keeling over and conking out for five minutes?'

'Did you go through as a bird?' asked Clive. 'Or a fox? Or otter? Or as a boy?'

'Just as a bird,' said Dax. 'Not much point in testing my other forms, is there? I'm hardly going to climb up an invisible dome and punch my way through it, am I?'

'No,' said Clive. 'But . . . there might be another way.'

12

Janet Marlow was excellent at her job. After twenty-five years with the Ministry Of Defence she had risen through the ranks and ended up working with some of the top men in Whitehall. There wasn't a more efficient, diligent, and trusted secretary in the whole civil service. Her last two years working with Forrester, running his London office, had been eye-opening to say the least. It wasn't until she was recruited by the COLA Project that she had any idea of the astonishing paranormal events that had been occurring across the country over the past five years, since the Children of Limitless Ability had first been discovered.

Of course, nothing she had ever read or seen in the dossiers would ever pass her lips; she had signed the Official Secrets Act in ink—but she would have signed it in her own blood if necessary. She was utterly committed to her job—she gave it her all. It cost her, though. She carried a lot of stress in her shoulders and in recent months her tension headaches had been getting more persistent. She had a real thumper rolling right now, in fact, which two paracetamol and three ibuprofen hadn't even dented.

She sat up straight in her chair, pushing the keyboard away and letting the contents of her screen drop out of

focus as she stretched her arms up and performed a little
office chair yoga. It was early evening and she'd been in
since 7 a.m. Everyone else had gone home. She would
too, just as soon as she'd finished tidying up Forrester's
latest report. As she dug her fingers into her scalp and
worked them through her short brown hair, a deep yawn
escaped her. The yawn sent a thrum through her head
which was why she didn't hear them arrive.

The first she knew of it was when her hand was taken
and a pulse of warmth shot up her arm. She gasped and
spun around in her chair. A girl was standing next to her,
dressed in a long white leather coat. Janet opened her
mouth to scream for security but the girl just smiled and
said 'No,' and the scream died in her throat. Panic was still
flapping away inside her chest like a caged wild bird but
she suddenly felt a whoosh of tingling and the complete
absence of pain in her head, neck, and shoulders. It left
her speechless. She had entirely forgotten what it felt like
to be living without pain.

'It's OK,' said the girl, fixing her with wide eyes of the
most beautiful violet blue. She was lovely. Just . . . lovely.
Her dark hair hung around her face in a jagged kind of
style and her smile felt like sun on Janet's skin. Somewhere
underneath all this wonder, the voice of twenty-five years'
experience and regular MOD security training was trying
to be heard. *You know who this is, don't you?* the voice said.

'Oh my God,' murmured Janet, staring up at those
eyes, surfing on wave after wave of joyous, painless
warmth. 'You're Mia Cooper.'

The girl smiled. 'You've heard of me? How nice! How are you feeling?'

'Good . . . so good,' sighed Janet. 'But worried. You really shouldn't be in here. Are you going to get your friend to take me away?' She glanced at the funky looking black kid with beaded dreadlocks who was leaning against the wall near the door.

'We don't have to,' said Mia. 'We'd have to cut the magnetite out of you first, wouldn't we? Olu can't teleport people with magnetite in their skin.' She ran her fingers across the squashy pad of flesh beneath Janet's left thumb where the magnetite lozenge had been inserted last year. 'And I wouldn't want to hurt you. I really don't like hurting people.'

'So . . . why are you here?'

'I need to know where my friends are,' said Mia.

'Your friends?'

'Yes. All the COLAs. They've been separated and moved around the country, haven't they?'

'It's for their own safety,' said Janet.

Mia sighed. 'Really, Janet? Just giving me the line you've been fed? You know the truth, don't you?'

'Well,' said Janet. 'It's about keeping everyone else safe, too. The new PM is jumpy.'

Mia laughed and it sounded like rain falling on a river. 'That's funny. Because he'll be a lot more jumpy soon. And that's nobody's fault but his. Now—Janet—I need you to show me where they've taken my friends.'

'You can't get in there,' said Janet. 'They've taken

precautions. They know all about you and Olu over there.'

'Wow,' said Olu. 'We're famous.' He looked unimpressed.

'Well, I didn't say I was going in there,' said Mia. 'I just need to know where they are.'

'I can't tell you,' said Janet. 'I really can't.'

Mia sighed and squeezed her hand. 'Do you know why you've been having headaches?' she asked.

Janet blinked. Had she told anyone about the headaches? She thought she'd totally hidden that. It would be so unprofessional to let people know. 'I get a bit tense across the shoulders,' she said.

'I bet you do,' said Mia. 'The things you've been allowed to know. But it's not that. You have a brain tumour.'

Fear stabbed through the blanket of warmth and joy she was being delightfully smothered in. She had sometimes thought, in the early hours of the morning, about dark things like this. An aunt had had a brain tumour. Died of it before Janet was ten.

'It's growing quite fast,' said Mia. 'I would give you six months, no more. Left without help. The doctors might make you last for eight or nine months. That's if you let them. The pain will be so bad in four months you'll probably just jump out of the window.' She glanced across at the floor-to-ceiling toughened glass that framed a view of the London skyline and a glimpse of the Thames in the setting sun.

Tears welled up in Janet's eyes and began to roll down her powdered cheeks. 'I don't want to die,' she said.

'Of course you don't. You have so much more to do. And Forrester would be lost without you,' added Mia. 'Janet, don't cry. Just show me what I need to know and I will take the tumour away. You do know, don't you, that I can do that? You've read the file?'

Janet nodded. She did know. She also knew what *else* Mia could do. 'I . . . I can't,' she whispered. 'Are you going to kill me?'

Mia shook her head, sadly. 'Janet, I don't need to kill you. You're dying anyway.'

She let go of Janet's hand and the pain flooded back so fast it felt like a blow from a jackhammer. Janet cried out and slumped onto her desk.

'I haven't made it worse,' said Mia. 'It's been terrible for days now, hasn't it? You've been so brave, carrying on with work like there's nothing wrong. I just gave you a break so you could remember how it felt to be pain-free.'

'Oh God, make it stop,' whimpered Janet. She felt as if her skull was being crushed in a vice. 'Please, make it stop.'

'I will,' said Mia. 'I will make it stop and I will save your life. *After* you have given me what I need. Don't worry. You don't have to feel bad. I'll take the tumour out and tweak your memory while I'm at it. You won't even remember we had this talk.'

Janet sat up, grabbed the keyboard, and rattled her

shaking fingers across it, making small animal noises of suffering.

Five minutes later Olu and Mia vanished and Janet awoke from a little doze, surprised at her lack of professionalism. And astonished at her lack of pain.

13

They waited until dawn. It was absurdly easy. Clive had an electronic pass card for areas of the science block and at 4 a.m., with only a skeleton staff on duty at the lodge, nobody challenged them as they crept out. Dax followed Clive as a fox, using his sharpened senses to keep them both away from any passing member of staff, but they only had to pause and wait once while somebody turned a corner and opened a door some distance from them.

When they reached the low brick building of the science block Dax shifted to falcon and Clive carefully tucked him inside his blue puffa jacket. No one but Clive would own such a ridiculous coat, thought Dax, pressed against his friend's neatly ironed grey shirt and almost deafened by his quick, nervous heartbeat. It looked like a boiler lagging jacket. But by now Clive's terrible taste in clothes was positively celebrated by the other COLAs who found it hilarious. Clive was puzzled by their reaction. 'It's comfortable,' he would protest. 'Why wouldn't I want to be comfortable?'

The laugh was on Dax right now, though, because when he shifted back to boy form he would be wearing some of Clive's pyjamas. They were faded *Star Trek* PJs. Clive had on some equally-faded pyjamas with *Firefly* written across the chest and the image of some kind of interstellar cowboy gang. 'No tracker chips,' Clive had told him, back in Dax's room, when he'd dug them out of a carrier bag. 'I traced them and removed them. Of course they're still in some of my clothes and shoes—I don't want to make an issue of it. But I'm not a COLA so the truth is, they're not really bothered about checking.'

Clive swiped his pass and went through a door. 'OK,' he murmured; his words rumbling through his chest into Dax's feathered head, 'We're in. It's crazy, isn't it? But the perimeter of this place is so well-guarded, nobody thinks there'll ever be an interloper this far in. And I'm *not* an interloper. I am allowed in—well, to certain places, anyway. I'm in at all hours, working on my projects. Of course, there will be camera evidence later—but I have a neat little trick for erasing the video. I'll show you sometime. And anyway, we're not stealing anything—just borrowing it.'

Eventually they came to the store room where Clive had seen the mobile rigs which created the test field Dax was made to fly through. In the low energy light, they looked like a couple of bulky tennis net stands, each on a wheeled base, with small rectangular boxes attached at chest height. There were tightly bound bright copper coils in each rectangular box and a series of switches below them.

'How will they power up?' Dax whispered, now out of Clive's puffa jacket and back to boy size.

'Battery packs,' said Clive, pointing to the square

metal boxes at the base. 'Come on—we need to get these outside. Can you block that with a wing or something?' Clive opened the door a crack and pointed to the security camera blinking a red light up in a corner of the dim corridor outside. 'So far they may have seen me come in to the store on my own—and that won't freak anyone out too much. I've done it before when I've been up all night on my projects. But if we start wheeling these things out they might get curious. If you can fly around the edge of this door, staying out of the camera's direct line of sight—and then flip across and block the view for a minute—well, that could be just a moth landing on it, couldn't it? And I could wheel these out and head out through the side door.'

'It's a plan,' said Dax. He was expecting alarms to go off and people to come running at any time but he followed Clive's suggestion and shifted to falcon. He went around the base of the door on talons, moving awkwardly across the polished floor of the corridor, keeping to the dim shadows. Then he flew up and arced around to the camera, landing on its slim bracket and putting a wing across the lens. It was not at all easy. He had nothing much to rest on and had to flap at high speed, like an insect, to stay aloft. At least his dark, thrumming underwing would look quite moth-like.

Meanwhile Clive had wheeled the rigs to the side door, swiped his pass card, and bumped them outside. He gave a low whistle and Dax flew off the camera with relief, swooping sideways, high along the corner where the wall met the ceiling and then flitting down just under the top of the door frame and out into the cool dawn. Back as a boy, he helped Clive to roll the rigs into the cover of some trees. It was still quite dark; thick cloud cover was keeping the dawn sun at bay. They found a small clearing and positioned the two rigs roughly four metres apart. Then Clive, after a cursory inspection, flipped some switches. The rigs hummed and whined through Dax's sensitive ears and he felt pins and needles assail his skin. The very earth under his bare feet seemed to recoil. He stepped back instinctively.

'What?' asked Clive, observing him keenly.

'Can't you hear it? Feel it?' said Dax.

Clive shrugged. 'Very low hum,' he said. 'That's all. Wasn't even sure it was *on* to start with.'

'It's on,' grunted Dax, already feeling ill.

'So—we won't make you fly through,' said Clive. 'We already know how that affects you and I can't be doing with you conking out in a pile of feathers.' He gave a sniff and then a sneeze. 'Did you know I'm allergic to you?' He blew his nose into a red cotton handkerchief. Yes—Clive carried cotton hankies too. Dax shook his head in wonder. 'I'm not so bad with the fox fur but the feathers really set off my rhinitis,' Clive burbled on. 'So—we need to know how you're affected in other forms. What's it to be first?'

Dax went to fox. He ran lightly across the dewy grass and turned, readying himself to cross the field. It sang even louder through his fox ears, like a crowd of deranged, shrieking people. His hackles rose. No animal would willingly approach this invisible barrier. He could sense them scurrying away from it in the grass below and the trees above.

He took a long breath and glanced at Clive. Clive actually had a small clipboard and pen in his hand. Where had he even been *keeping* that?! Dax took a breath and ran for the barrier. As he reached it the shrieking in his ears rose in a sickly crescendo but he did not flinch. He pelted through and immediately felt his consciousness desert him, as if he'd been struck on the temple with a spade. He spasmed and rolled across the grass. Blackness took him.

He awoke to find Clive crouching over him, glancing at a stopwatch. His first words were 'Sixty three seconds,' and then 'Are you OK?' He was back in boy form, slumped on his side and shivering in the *Star Trek* pyjamas. He crawled a yard or two through the grass and threw up what little he'd eaten last night. He did his best to wipe a little splash-back off Captain Kirk's face.

'Sorry, old chap!' said Clive. 'But it's better than your last attempt. As a falcon you were out of it for nearly three minutes, according to the data I've checked.'

Dax didn't bother to ask Clive how he had checked. The boy was a mystery to him. An enigma.

'Try again as soon as you're feeling OK,' said Clive. He eyed the science block between the trees. 'But don't take too long—the first team usually starts at 6 a.m. It's 5.12 now.'

Next Dax went through as an otter. The effect was very similar and he was out cold for fifty-one seconds. Was an otter stronger than a fox? Or was he just getting very slightly used to the field? It didn't feel that way as he retched into a ditch.

'Now,' said Clive, his voice a register lower—as if the first two attempts were a warm-up act to the main show. 'Time to go through in human form. I suggest you run again. You want to expose yourself for as little time as possible. The electromagnetic beam is only fifty-three centimetres across. Get through it fast.'

Dax walked back from the rigs and steadied his breathing, pushing away the nausea. He summoned the animal part of him—the hunter—and felt a strengthening somewhere below his ribcage.

He ran for the barrier and heard its shriek again—but not so loud through human ears. He swept through the beam and fell face-first into the grass, twitching. Faintness came for him but he drove it back and raised his head. 'Twelve seconds,' said Clive, crouching over him with the stopwatch. 'Just as I thought. Not calibrated for human physiology and brainwaves. But twelve seconds is not good enough. You need to go again.'

'What?' groaned Dax, rolling onto his back and rubbing his tingling face.

'Again. You need to train—to get used to the feeling. Cut down your black-out time.'

'I didn't black out this time.'

'Yes you did—but not for long. How long do you think it would take a human to drop one hundred metres?'

'Without wind? In free fall? About six or seven seconds.'

'That's what I thought. So you can only be out for four seconds,' said Clive, tapping his small pen against his teeth. 'Then you'll have to shift back to bird, pull up, and avoid the ground—or maybe only two seconds because you'll be going through at a lower angle.'

'Are you suggesting that I fly one hundred metres up and then shift back to a boy?' Dax sat up and peered at his friend. 'You're nuts.'

'The dome is at least one hundred metres high,' said Clive. 'You would know more about that than I would. But you can't fly that high and shift because you'd simply drop. No—this is all about optimum trajectory and velocity. You'd need to build up speed, perhaps on a circular route, and then approach the field at the highest point possible before you shift. Ideally on the southern perimeter where the ground slopes away steeply on the other side—that might buy you a second or two more. Your aerodynamics will instantly drag you down, of course, so you need enough velocity to get clear of the outer curve before you fall—so in fact you'll need to exit at quite a low point; which will cut down your recovery time. It's difficult . . . but not impossible. Let me do the maths while you have another go. This time, fly at the barrier but shift back to boy form at the last moment. And try to stay aerodynamic!'

Dax shook his head. 'You're off the scale insane.' But he got up and did as Clive suggested, flying at the barrier and then hurtling through it as a boy, his arms and legs tucked back straight, in the arrow shape the bird had been. He dug a small furrow in the grass and leaf litter with his face. But he was only out for seven seconds this time. And he wasn't sick. Incredibly, he seemed to be getting used to the field.

They had five more attempts and the fourth was the best. He shifted from falcon to boy at the very last microsecond, as he felt his avian brain begin to warp, and managed to reach the other side in boy form, facebutt the ground again, and regain consciousness in six seconds. The fifth go saw no improvement; in fact he was a second slower to recover.

'You're getting exhausted now. We have to stop,' said Clive. 'But this is brilliant. You can do this. Only . . . for the perfect drop with the right parabolic curve, your optimum intersect point with the dome will have to be really quite low—not far above the fence. Which means your drop time is too short . . . unless . . . Look—leave it with me. I can work this out.'

They rolled the rigs back to the science block in silence, Clive deep in calculations and Dax too tired to speak or even think. He wasn't sure what they had achieved here. A long-winded route to a spectacular suicide maybe?

They repeated the process of blocking the camera as Clive returned the rigs to the store room. It was all Dax could do to stay up there. His brain was aching and his light bird limbs felt leaden. But they pulled it off. Nobody stopped them as they returned, Dax once again under the puffa jacket. It was true—they must be focusing all their attention on the perimeter. Or maybe Clive had interfered with the system somehow. Dax didn't doubt that he was capable. At the lodge he summoned enough strength to fly up to his open window. He was in bed thirty seconds later and asleep ten seconds after that.

14

He dreamed of Gideon and Luke. They were being kept in some kind of giant concrete silo. There was no daylight, just a single bare bulb hung on a flex which dangled down ten or fifteen metres from the ceiling—or lid—of the silo.

Gideon was so angry he wanted to smash the bulb and Dax was begging him not to because then he would be in the dark. Then he dreamed of a bus driver wearing an elephant's trunk and Lisa lying asleep underwater.

He woke up sweating and knotted in his sheets. 'I had this dr—' he began, before he realized that there was nobody to tell it to. Gideon's bed was empty. Someone had stripped the sheets and duvet and pillows off it and taken them away.

He sank on to his back and ran his fingers through his damp hair. *LISA!* he sent. *Where are you?* Nothing came back. Did that mean Lisa was in trouble? He couldn't be sure. His telepathic connection with her was patchy at a distance. Usually it only worked well if she had made a deliberate connection with him, especially when he was a fox. Maybe she liked him best that way. He shifted now and curled his tail around him, sending out another call. *LISA! Can you hear me? Where are you?*

Why did he need to ask? Forrester had been plain enough. She was somewhere new. And she wasn't coming back.

Dax felt a wave of anger and frustration. Adrenalin began to pump through him. He could NOT stay here. He HAD to get away. So . . . did he trust Clive's barmy idea about flying through the dome—as a boy? It was one hell of a calculated risk. He'd taken risks before but was he desperate enough—or brave enough—to take this one?

Before breakfast he flew around the perimeter, as close to the field as he could manage without getting foggy and sick. Clive was right about the southern end. It was hard to see now, because he could not fly above the perimeter itself any more; the inward curve of the dome made that impossible. But he could see enough to locate the spot where the land fell away in a craggy drop. One of the rivers which crossed the estate flowed fast through its new metal gate and he could hear it thundering in a waterfall just out of his sight. If he exited here, the drop would give him an extra second or two.

And then what? Where would he go? Lisa and Gideon could be anywhere in the country.

He flew back to the lodge and joined the other Cat. B COLAs for breakfast. It was a quiet affair. The shock and anger of yesterday had given way to a depression. Perhaps each of them was now beginning to understand how controlled and manipulated their lives were. Jennifer sat close to Barry and periodically dropped her head into her hands, her bowl of cereal largely untouched. At one point she looked at Dax across the table and gave him a thin smile. 'I'm so glad you're still here with us,' she said. 'It feels like there's hardly anyone left.' Dax smiled back and reached across to take her hand but she vanished before their fingers met. He could hear her quiet crying, though, as she left the room. Barry got up and followed her and Jacob and Alex exchanged bleak looks over their toast.

Dax had not felt rage like this for a long time—not since before his shapeshifter days; back when he was only a kid, living with his half-sister and a stepmum who had no liking for him. Back then he had carried so much burnt out anger inside him, like hot lava turned to stone, he was weighed down with it. He had almost forgotten that feeling. Maybe it was back for good now. If he didn't do something.

There was a movie day running. The remaining staff at the lodge—all newer staff who had less of a connection with the COLAs, Dax noticed—had set up a cinema in the hall, with a giant screen and seating for all thirty-four of them. They were running Marvel movies back-to-back and handing out fizzy drinks and popcorn.

Some of the COLAs went with it; others looked inside at the effort that had been made to cheer them up, muttered, 'Seriously?', and walked away. The audience peaked at twenty.

Dax discovered a letter from Alice in his pigeonhole in the school office. He sighed as he took it to his room.

He had been dropping hints to Alice for some time now about how things were getting bad at COLA Club, but Alice was thirteen and obsessed with herself and her own life. How likely was it she'd pick up his hidden messages? He remembered his last attempt and wondered if she truly believed he watched *Celebrity Cellmates*. Was she really that dim?

It seemed she was. The letter opened with great excitement about their shared passion for the show.

LOL! You're finally getting into Celeb Cellmates! It's brilliant isnt it? Jazmeena SO needs to dump Slap DeFace. Life at schools OK. I'm doing dance now and I'm prob the best one there. Mum bought me four pairs of leather jazz shoes. They are SOOOO kool. LOL.

Dax sighed. He knew Alice wasn't stupid but she seemed to have traded most of her brain for a box of sequins. He read through quickly as she wittered on about how amazing it would be to be famous, skipping over her dreadful spelling, and trying not to judge. But then his eyes screwed up and he re-read a paragraph. What was she going on about now?

I could just live in a giant manshon with 500 acres and employ a team of gaurds to keep people out if I didn't feel like talking to them

That was a bit close to his world.

Me and Mina both do dance and she says she'll come to stay at the manshon and there'll have to be a river so her dad and brother can come and fish in it. They are bonkers about fishing. I think it's sooooooo boring but Mina says it's good to sit next to a fisher because they give you hedspace. Their like Zen or something

This was weird. Since when did Alice think about 'headspace' or Zen? This Mina must be having some influence! But something else prickled in his mind. Fisher. Fisher. *Fisher.*

And then there was the next bit . . .

Got to go. Tiana is coming round to tell me about the latest Dylan drama. She keeps getting back together with him and then breaking up and then getting back . . . she's bonkers. She'll go back to that ex moor than any sane person should!

Fisher. Ex moor . . . *go back to that ex moor . . .*

Caroline Fisher. Exmoor. Was he imagining this?!

Dax felt the hairs stand up all over his skin. He shook his head and muttered: 'Alice Jones—you have got to be kidding me!'

If he was not mistaken, his airheaded little sister had just sent him a coded message. A place he could go for help. Of course he *couldn't* go there. Caroline Fisher's place in Exmoor was where he and the others had run last time when they were in crisis. If he ran again, the very *first* place the Project would check would be The Owl Box.

And yet ... Caroline must have some plan—for clearly it was Caroline who was communicating with him alongside Alice. He grinned as he imagined what must have happened. Alice *had* picked up his code. She *had* understood. He felt bad for underestimating her. So, knowing that their dad would not be much help—and Alice's mum, Gina, would be worse than useless—she had thought about someone who could help and remembered the journalist, Caroline Fisher. Alice would only have been eight when the whole business with Caroline Fisher happened down in Cornwall. How had she remembered?

OK—stop marvelling and start working this out, he told himself. Why would Caroline suggest he go back to The Owl Box? She must know it was not safe—not a second time. Maybe there was something else going on, though. It would not hurt to at least scout the area out. See what he could see.

Dax put the letter on the bed and stared out of the window into the blue summer sky. He had a direction. South west. He suddenly realized that Clive's barmy idea to escape the dome was no longer a barmy idea. It was a plan.

He would spend his last day at Fenton Lodge eating

and relaxing. He would go down and watch back-to-back Marvel movies, stuff his face with sweet popcorn, and then eat the biggest lunch, tea, and dinner he could. He needed to fuel himself up for the flight of his life. Or his death.

15

'Are you actually going to do it?' hissed Clive as *X-Men: Days of Future Past* flickered energetically across the screen.

'I don't know,' lied Dax. 'I'm thinking about it. That's all. Maybe it's stupid. Where would I go?'

Clive didn't answer. They both knew where Dax would go. To find Lisa and Gideon and Luke. 'Don't tell me,' he said. 'I don't want to know anything else. They might get one of the mind readers on to me . . . except there are none left here any more.'

Dax could think of other ways they could make Clive talk. He did not share this thought as the boy pressed a folded piece of paper into his hands. 'This is the maths,' he muttered. 'And a diagram.'

Dax shoved it in his pocket. In the gloom of the temporary cinema he was pretty sure the staff had not noticed. 'I'm probably not going,' he lied, again. 'Don't worry.'

He wanted to add: 'And if I do and they find me in pieces, it's not your fault, Clive.' But this wouldn't help either.

After dinner he went to his room and opened the paper. The diagram on it showed a perfectly-drawn dome, one hundred metres at its highest point, and an angle of intersect; the best possible point at which Dax might break through and still survive. Clive had written compass bearings and noted: *You will have a maximum of seven seconds but only if you cross the southern perimeter above the waterfall. You MUST cross here. First fly high, circle, build up speed and then stoop to get maximum velocity. Drop as far as you dare and then flip and use the momentum to slingshot yourself through at a forty-five degree angle (this might gain you an extra second). You must exit the dome no higher than ten metres above the fence. If there is even light wind DO NOT attempt this. You will have to go naked. I can't let my* Star Trek *PJs go.*

Dax laughed out loud.

Please destroy this information.

He read it three more times, and then ate it.

16

Sgt Sean Jeffery was on duty in Checkpoint Five on the southern flank of the perimeter.

Like all the soldiers recruited to guard Fenton Lodge for the COLA Project, his chief concern was keeping potential hostiles from getting *into* the grounds.

But he had also been trained to watch for something which might come *out*. A falcon. It would be dazed and falling. They were ready with a hot button to call an emergency response the second they saw any such thing. The button had been pressed seven times since the new dome system had been activated two weeks ago. On each occasion the emergency response team had quickly ascertained that the COLA boy was safe in the lodge or the grounds. The victim was just a hapless pigeon or rook; too old or lame to avoid the field. Ninety-nine point nine per cent of the estate's birdlife had the birdbrain to stay put inside the vast projected dome and not tangle with it. Animal sense counted for more than most people would think; without it there would be an ugly pile-up of rotting carcasses in a grim faerie ring around the fells and meadows—and a lot of freaked-out kids alerting their dads. (Apparently none of the COLA's had living mothers—another very unsettling fact.)

No—the birds had shown admirable intelligence. And so far, so had the shapeshifter boy.

Dax Jones, he was called, and he looked normal enough on the posters inside the checkpoints. Dark haired, dark-eyed lad, mixed-race; ordinary. Not tall, not short—lean and wiry and fit—kind of handsome. Girls probably went for him, thought Sgt Jeffery, emptying a sugar sachet and stirring his coffee as he glanced again at the poster. You'd never guess what he was by looking at him and many of the soldiers found it hard to believe. How could a teenage boy turn into a bird? Or a fox? Or an otter? How was that possible? Where did ten stone of flesh and bone go when he shifted into a falcon no bigger than a crow?! And what about all his clothes and stuff? Apparently they just shifted with him. It made no sense.

What the other COLA kids could do was also legend by now but somehow this shapeshifting boy just blew all the laws of physics. If it was even true.

He shook his head again; it made a normal person's mind do backflips. Anyway—the perimeters and the dome were doing their job, so he probably never would see this legendary bird. He glanced at the monitors in the small room. There were twelve such huts around the perimeter of the estate and in each of them a bored guard sat, watching the screens for blips in the electronics, spikes in the seismographs, and old school video surveillance for the naked eye.

Nothing. Almost always nothing. And now, since the dome, seven times nothing. Certainly no dazed bird falling to Earth and landing as a broken boy. Kid would be insane to try it.

He circled three times. Faster and faster, the fells below beginning to blur in the dim dawn light. He wished Gideon could be on the ground, giving him a telekinetic push and doubling his speed . . . but if Gideon were here, he wouldn't be attempting this. Or perhaps he would. To find Lisa . . .

The invisible dome sang its hideous song, making his whole body buzz with dread. Was he *really* going to do this? It might be the last decision he ever made.

If Sgt Jeffery hadn't taken two sugars he would have seen something utterly baffling. Had he been watching his screens, instead of rooting around in his drawer for a second sachet to put in his coffee, he would have seen a blip on the dome read-out. Just a blip—not an alarm; for the interruption carried no bird signature. More importantly he would have seen something on the video feed—something shooting through the air, above the trees, about to intersect with the invisible curve of the dome just above it.

By the time the electronic alarms on the four-metre-high walls went off, jerking every sentinel in every checkpoint, into action, he was way too late to see a teenage boy hurtle through the air, naked as a newborn, on a collision course for certain death on the rocky fell below.

✳ ✳ ✳

' . . . three . . . two . . . one . . . BOY!'

The abrupt loss of aerodynamics lurched through him. At once he pulled his arms and legs in and rolled in the thin air. He knew he would drop but at this trajectory his velocity should still carry him through.

He felt the prickle of the electromagnetic dome pass through him and at once his mind fizzed and spun— but stayed conscious. The training had *worked*. But his success would be short-lived if he didn't sharpen up and shift back to bird again in four seconds. Dax fell. And fell. His legs and arms clawed at the air and a cry of panic escaped him as he tipped, head first, into the final two seconds of his life. A large pale crown of rock reached for him. Its crags and corners threw themselves up like welcoming arms amid the blue-green of the moss and grass. *Come to me! Let me kiss your face! Spread your body and soul across me for one perfect moment before you quit this world!*

17

He got his shift together a blink away from that rocky kiss. Transforming, flipping up; cheating gravity with a bird-pitched cry of relief; unable to stop himself. Then he shot, like a dark-feathered arrow, straight for the churning ribbon of dark water that gushed out from under the perimeter, through a grid of iron.

If flying as a boy had seemed terrifyingly wrong, diving into water as a falcon seemed no better. But when they discovered he'd gone and found no broken body on the perimeter, they'd search the skies first. There was a chance they might not think about the river for a while. They might not imagine he would *swim* away.

Spinning through the thick slow water, he felt his falcon frame shudder with shock, but a second later he had shifted to the otter and now he was borne along, slick as a salmon, in the unstoppable current. He stayed low, far beneath the surface, holding his breath effortlessly for the first four minutes—and with somewhat more effort for another sixty seconds. Then he pelted into a curved eddy of weed and tree root at the edge of the river and allowed his nostrils to rise clear just long enough to fuel another five minutes of submergence.

He was built for this. He could go on this way for

hours. All night. Until he was far enough away to risk flying again.

A frisson of delight spread through his limbs as he powered on down through the river's depths and rode the current southward. The river would hide him, give him safe passage, food, and protection. He could remain an otter indefinitely if he chose. In fact he could live wild and never be troubled by any human again.

He loved to be wild.

Awkwardly, he also loved certain humans.

18

Caroline Fisher chose the guest house mostly because it was a short distance from a very good hiding place for her Toyota. It was late and she hoped the owners would still be up and willing to accommodate her. After hiding out in the Toyota for three days, watching and waiting with her binoculars at the ready, she had finally given in to the lure of a bath and a bed. There was no hope of spotting a peregrine falcon at night anyway. She'd be back on watch again by dawn the next day. Probably. She'd give it one more day before she admitted it was a wild goose chase.

But even while one voice in her head insisted that Dax Jones was probably perfectly fine and sleeping comfortably back at Fenton Lodge with no *real* plan to escape, another one wouldn't let her give in just yet. She just *felt* that something was coming. And she had begun to worry, as she drove back up to the main road, that the car would give her away. Its registration plates were in her name. As she drove off in search of a hotel she realized she should ditch the Toyota if she was going to carry on with this daft plan. That's when another idea came to her and she drove a little further north with a particular seaside village in mind, found the parking spot under thick tree cover, and walked to the guest house.

Happily the nice couple who ran it were content to be paid in cash and didn't push for ID. She played it ditzy and said she'd left her purse, with all her cards, on the train, then signed in as Emma Fitzgerald from Bristol, giving a fake address and contact number.

She wanted to get back to her lookout by dawn but it might have to be slightly later than that. She had a new plan which might delay her. As she sank into a warm bath with a groan of relief, she hoped if Dax showed up at daybreak he would have the sense to wait a while. She wasn't superhuman!

But he probably wouldn't show up anyway.

19

Dax had to stop. He surfaced, his nostrils and ears opening with his eyes, and a glance at the bright sky confirmed he'd been swimming with the current for more than four hours. He was exhausted. He landed on the bank of a bend in the river, deep in a wooded valley. Had he swum far enough?

He needed to eat. But he needed to sleep more. He lifted his blunt brown snout and shook drops off its spray of whiskers as he scented the air. There was no territorial dog otter close enough to worry about. But there might be a holt or a fox's den he could borrow. Or he could shift back into falcon form and roost up in the branches. No. No, he was too tired to shift again right now. Climbing wearily onto the bank, he followed his nose and discovered some old spraints; crumbly otter leavings that marked a route towards a holt—an underground cavern accessed from the riverbank. That was what he needed. But would it be vacant?

Again, he relied upon scent to guide him. The holt *had* been occupied, probably only a few days ago. But it was empty now. He slipped back into the water and ducked under to find the access point. A small dark hole beneath a knotted tree root beckoned him in. He swam through the tight tunnel for a few metres before it arched upwards and he was suddenly clear of the water in a small earth cave. He could immediately scent a female and her young but realized at once that they were gone. The mother had probably moved her kits to another location a few days ago.

Left behind was a bed of dry grass and a few vole bones. To Dax it was as welcoming as a hotel. He curled into the bedding, feeling as relieved as any human sinking under a clean duvet in an en suite room.

His aching muscles slowly powered down but for a long time sleep escaped him. He could picture the scientists back at the lodge, desperately trying to trace him. Would they have found his chipped clothes yet? He had buried them deep inside an abandoned badger sett. He guessed that the sett would be dug up as they tried to work out whether he was down there, curled up as a fox or otter (he had slept this way a few times before) or whether he'd really escaped, leaving his chipped clothing behind.

It drove them crazy that they couldn't chip his skin. They had tried this a few years ago and the result was catastrophic—nearly killing all eleven of the COLAs in their care. The resulting fall out and investigation had forced the COLA Project to legally commit to never interfering with the COLAs' bodies in any way again, without written permission from their families.

But they had tried everything else they could think of to keep control. They even chipped underwear and swimming gear. The constant buzz of the tiny metal transmitters connecting with the tracking equipment was like tinnitus in Dax's head. Some of the other more sensitive COLAs could pick it up too. Nobody liked it but most accepted the line that it was for their own good. Ever since they had been discovered and brought together more than five years ago, the COLAs had endured attacks and attempts at abduction. In the event of another such attempt, Forrester reassured them, they would be trackable—instantly.

As long as they kept their clothes on. Dax wondered how many families had now given consent to have their teenagers chipped under the skin . . . just in case. After all, they'd all agreed to magnetite beads being inserted into their palms just last year. This was to prevent Olu, a rogue COLA, from seizing them and teleporting them away—a terrifying thought which meant the families didn't need much persuading. Now some of them were thinking a tracker chip wasn't so different.

Dax knew it was but he didn't expect the others to understand. So yes, by now, his chipped clothes had probably been dug up and the scientists were in meltdown, trying to work out how he had escaped the electromagnetic dome. Forrester would be seething. The otter allowed itself a fangy grin at the thought. If Chambers had still been in charge he would have had some hope of finding his lost COLA. He understood Dax and how he thought.

Dax sighed, drifting slightly closer to sleep but still

unable to let go. Where was Chambers now? What had happened to him?

The last time Dax had seen him, Chambers had told him he was off to see the new Prime Minister. He hadn't said anything about leaving. And Dax was sure he *would* have told him, if he'd known what was to happen.

A week later Forrester arrived and took possession of Chambers's office. His first meeting with Dax had not been friendly.

'You live in a paradise here, Jones,' Forrester had said. 'Luxury. Your every need is catered for—even down to allowing you complete freedom to roam this estate. No other COLA enjoys that privilege. Please don't do anything to make me withdraw that privilege.'

And then the security 'improvements' had begun.

Next came Forrester's test to prove that Dax could not pass through the electromagnetic field he was setting up; a clear statement that he was no longer trusted to stay within the grounds. It was all very sophisticated. Only one thing had escaped the clever new head of the Project—Clive. Forrester was so caught up in the threat from his COLA charges that he'd totally underestimated the one kid with no 'powers' at all.

Dax chuckled to himself as he at last fell asleep.

20

She found the old garage looking exactly the same as she'd last seen it. And Seth, her old boyfriend, looking exactly the same as she'd last seen him. Apart from the expression of shock that she'd got him out of bed before 8 a.m.

'Hello, Seth.'

'Caro!' he burbled, stubbly and confused. 'It's been ages! What are you doing here?'

'Collecting an IOU,' she said, with a smile. 'Remember when I talked the editor of the *Falmouth Packet* out of covering your court case?'

He grinned. 'I am eternally grateful.'

'Grateful enough to lend me a bike?'

He looked uneasy. 'The Triumph?'

'Yup.' She'd always ridden the Triumph when they'd been together.

He sighed and peered along towards the garage beneath his tiny flat. Its door was beautifully painted— angel wings above a skull.

'Nice work.' Caroline arched an eyebrow.

'It took me a week,' he said. Seth was an artist—and a committed Hell's Angel biker. He made some money from painting and more from doing up the bikes of his fellow chapter members. 'So . . . this bike loan. How long?'

'A couple of days probably,' she said. 'Oh . . . and I'll need my old leathers and helmet, if you haven't flogged them. And a pair of good binoculars.'

'You don't want much, do you?' he grumbled, but he was smiling. They'd had good times.

Ten minutes later she was in her old gear and astride the Triumph Tiger Explorer; a gleaming monster of chrome and leather with a 1215cc three cylinder engine which purred and growled.

'I hope you get your scoop,' he said as she throttled up.

'It's not a story,' she said.

Seth pushed back his shock of fuzzy brown hair and narrowed his eyes. 'What are you getting yourself into, Caro?' he asked. 'Are you in trouble?'

'I'm fine,' she said. 'But if anyone asks . . . you didn't see me.'

'You *are* in trouble, aren't you?'

Caroline remembered how caring he'd been. Frustrating, unreliable, and daft . . . but always caring.

'It's nothing I can't handle,' she said. It was something she said to herself almost daily. 'I'll bring her back to you.' And she sped off with a roar.

21

Alice couldn't concentrate. Tiana was sprawled on her bed, going on and on about her boyfriend woes. Usually Alice would be loving it—lapping up all the drama—but today who said what on Facebook and who replied on Gosso and who sent a stupid photo on ClikTrik seemed like a very small deal. Especially after the calls. The silent calls. Number withheld.

There had been three of them in the past twenty-four hours. One on her mobile and two on the landline. Maybe more . . . Mum might have picked some up but she hadn't mentioned them if so. It wasn't some sales thing, either. Silent sales calls had give-away clicks and sometimes even background noise from a call centre just before someone launched into their pitch. Often the sales messages were recorded and you could pretty much hear the machinery relaying the message: 'We have been trying to reach you urgently regarding your claim . . .'

But this was different. There was no voice, no click, no atmosphere at all except . . . *listening*. She knew they were listening. To her. After her initial hello she had tried again and got no reply. Then she made a stupid mistake. One word. She said 'Dax . . . ?' and then the coldness had spread through her chest. Whoever it was, they never hung up first. They just listened. Waited. Until she slammed down the phone in panic.

' . . . chatting up Carrie Mortimer because she's been all over him like a rash!' Tiana didn't seem to notice how quiet Alice was. She'd been on motormouth mode since yesterday teatime, when she'd come for a sleepover. It was amazing how she could just keep rolling out the news like a daytime TV presenter. Mina was Alice's preferred friend, really. She didn't have all the latest gossip but she didn't talk non-stop either. Still, Tiana could be fun . . . when Alice was in the right mood. And today she really wasn't. 'Carrie thinks she is so cool but she's just a flirt. So anyway, I thought I'd go and chat up Tom just to get Dylan's back up and I could see he was looking over at me and he was getting annoyed and . . . look, here's some video . . .'

The landline rang out from downstairs and Alice jolted. This was really getting to her!

The ringing cut off as Mum picked up and Alice waited, totally tuned out of Tiana's latest episode of teen drama. She heard Mum murmuring and then 'ALICE! Can you come down here?'

Tiana paused the video on her phone and rolled her eyes.

'Sorry,' said Alice. 'Better see what she wants *now* . . .' Tiana gave an elaborate sigh and plucked her headphones out of her bag, instantly locking in to her favourite band with closed eyes and rhythmic head jerks as she lay back on Alice's pink bedspread.

Mum was in the kitchen, having a late breakfast, still in her quilted orange robe.

'I've got Jennifer on speakerphone,' she said, closing the kitchen door. 'She wants to speak to us both. Where's Tiana?'

'She upstairs with headphones on,' said Alice. 'Hi, Jennifer. What's up?'

Jennifer was their COLA Project Liaison Officer. She stayed in touch with them about Dax's progress reports up in Cumbria and other matters that arose concerning him. When Dad was home he dealt with Jennifer one-to-one, but when he was away on the oil rigs he was sometimes hard to reach and his second wife had to handle the calls. Mum would far rather concentrate on her daughter and herself and forget Dax even existed—but as Alice now knew, their very comfortable lifestyle was down to her stepson being a COLA, so Mum had to make some kind of effort for the CPLO.

'Hi, Alice. Look—I don't want you to worry, either of you,' Jennifer said, her voice emanating from the landline phone, set down on the side. 'It's just that Dax went out for a wander in the night. It's not unusual and we don't stop him, as you know—it's part of how we manage his condition,' she added, as if shapeshifting was an illness. 'But so far, he hasn't come back.'

'Oh,' Mum said, drizzling honey on her waffles beside the toaster. 'So . . . he's flown off somewhere. I expect he'll come back when he's hungry.'

There was a slightly nervous half-chuckle in

response. 'Well, yes, except with his—er—talents, he can feed himself pretty well.'

Mum visibly shuddered. 'Haven't you got him chipped or something?' she said, pouring herself some coffee.

'No—his father wouldn't allow it,' said Jennifer. 'Most of the COLA fathers have refused, Gina, since that . . . situation . . . a couple of years ago.'

'Well, they're idiots,' said Mum. 'These kids should always be tracked. God knows what they might do.'

'Anyway, we think there may be a chance he'll come to you,' said Jennifer.

'Why?' snapped Mum, suddenly eyeing the window nervously. 'He's never been here before. He sees his dad up at the COLA place.'

'Even so . . . just in case. He is in touch with Alice, after all.'

Mum swung around and looked at her, surprised. 'Is he?'

Alice shrugged. 'Birthday cards . . . a letter once in a while.' Her heart was beating fast.

'Alice—have you heard from Dax recently?' asked Jennifer.

There was no point in lying. 'Had a letter from him last week,' said Alice. 'Sent him one on . . . Friday, I think.'

'Was there anything in the letter that might help us?'

As if they hadn't already read it. 'He's got the hots for Jazzmeena,' Alice said.

'Jazzmeena?'

Alice clicked her teeth and gave it her best vapid, unimpressed response: 'You know—the one who was in *Celebrity Cellmates*?! Got married to Slap DeFace? Massive boob job?'

'Oh—*that* Jazzmeena. OK . . . well, if there's anything else you can think of; any clue to what was on his mind or where he might have gone . . . it would really help to know.'

'We'll call you right away if we find out anything,' said Mum. After the call she turned to face her daughter. 'I didn't know you've been writing to Dax.'

Alice shrugged. ''S'no big deal.'

'But you have *nothing* in common with him. Why would you bother?'

Alice stared at her. 'He's my brother. And even if *you* hate him, I don't.'

'I don't want you encouraging him to come here,' said Mum, her nostrils flaring and her small eyes widening. Red blotches appeared across her fleshy throat. 'He does NOT belong here; do you understand me?'

'He's my brother,' repeated Alice. 'He's a blood relative!'

'You don't want *any* of that blood,' said Mum with a shudder.

Alice stalked out of the kitchen. 'He wouldn't be caught dead in this place, anyway!' she snapped. 'And I don't blame him!'

'He's dangerous!' Mum yelled after her as she ran upstairs. 'I don't want him coming anywhere near you!

Or any of his other freak friends!'

Alice ignored her and slammed her bedroom door as soon as she was back in. Tiana took off her headphones. 'Your mum being a cow again?' she asked, face full of sympathy.

'She's *always* a cow!' said Alice. She picked up her phone and peered at it. There were some messages from friends on ClikTrik—at least half of them from Tiana despite the fact she was here in the same room. What *else* was on her phone? Aside from all the messages and posts and photos and texts . . . there was a SIM card which informed the network exactly where she was at any time. It was a gift, really, from those nice COLA Project people. And a gift *to* them.

Alice looked at Tiana, lounging on her bed. It was almost a mirror image. They both had the same long straight hair, light brown or dark blonde depending on the weather and what they wore. Today they were both in skinny jeans and little cotton tops. They both had bangles and friendship bracelets clinking on their wrists and they both had exactly the same expensive lace-up trainers on. They were the same height and build; people often took them for sisters.

Alice pressed the mute option. If a call came through it wouldn't be heard. She deactivated the vibrate mode too. The phone was on, but still and silent.

'Sorry, Tee,' sighed Alice. 'But I think you'd better go. Mum's really getting worked up and it's probably better if you don't hang around.'

Tiana sat up and pouted. 'But I've got loads more to tell you!' she whined, pushing her lower lip out. 'Can't you just say sorry or something?'

'No—you heard her shrieking, didn't you? She's being a total cow.'

Tiana sighed. 'I'll get my things.' She went into the en suite shower room to collect her toothbrush and stuff and while she was gone Alice lost no time in opening her friend's little purple overnight bag and shoving her phone right to the bottom of it. Five minutes later she was seeing Tiana out. She took care to stand back from the door, out of sight.

Tiana called 'Byeee!' loudly as she went. Luckily she didn't shout, 'Byeee, Alice!' or, 'Byeee, Mrs Jones.' Just the one 'Byeee' and that was fine.

Alice felt guilty as she shut the door and slunk back up to her room. What kind of friend was she?

Along the well-manicured street in what Caroline had referred to as Rich Toffsville, a phone company van was parked at the kerb. Inside it the man with the headset radioed in. 'Alice Jones is on the move.'

'Follow discreetly,' came back Control.

'Will we be picking her up?'

'Just follow for now . . . see where she's going. And keep watch for a bird. Or a fox. Or—if she goes to the river—'

'Yeah, I know,' said the headset man. 'An otter.'

22

Hunger woke him after four or five hours' sleep. He stretched his limbs and felt the ache of his long swim. He was fit and used to plenty of exercise but he had never swum that far before. He had more than burned off all the food he'd eaten yesterday.

Dax nosed out of the holt, scenting the air for humans or other otters. He could smell neither. Although the sun was high in the sky, his sheltered stretch of the river was under thick tree canopy. Midges danced in the tiny dappled pools of light which broke through the leaves and an unwary trout snapped its round wet mouth at the surface. Dax felt hunger pulse through him and he slid into the water like a stealth missile. Two minutes later he was under the overhanging roots at the entrance to the holt, ripping the fish apart while its tail still thudded reflexively. Some small part of him hoped the creature did not suffer—but a far larger part of him did not care. This meal was essential. Delicious too.

Although it was day and he should probably travel by night he felt desperate to push on and put more miles between himself and Fenton Lodge. Should he keep swimming or was it safe to take flight? For a while he could not decide and so he flitted through the thick woodland alongside the river as a fox. His sense of smell was keenest in this form and it was easy to keep well clear of people who occasionally tramped through the woods. He snacked on insects as he went, snapping up beetles and spiders like he'd snapped up popcorn the day before.

Eventually he reached the end of the dark veil of forest. The river rolled on across undulating pastureland, now reflecting the high blue sky. Dax did not roll on with it. He paused. It was time. He could wait until dark but that was still hours away and falcons did not fly well by night; they were not built for it.

How far did the COLA Project have eyes on the sky? They could not possibly watch everywhere and even if he was spotted by some birdwatcher, he looked exactly like any other wild peregrine tiercel.

He shifted and flew instinctively in a wide arc as his avian brain calculated direction from the planet's natural magnetism and the sun's place in the sky. He needed to go south west. He had no map but the precise shape and pattern of the land he was heading for was burned into his memory. He thought he could be there in two hours; maybe sooner.

The English countryside unfolded beneath him in a haze of gold, green, and blue. He had forgotten how glorious it was to be so free. His journey was joyous. He was acutely aware of the ever-shifting landscape below and the occasional panicky dives among flocks of pigeons who noticed the dark arrow of death soaring above them. He felt as if he belonged; as much a part of this element as the white vapour of the clouds and the warmth of the rising thermals; a bird woven into a tapestry of sky; of it, in it, from it, for it.

2 3

Alice watched through the blinds as Tiana trotted off down the street. The white telephone company van started up a few seconds after she passed it and Alice felt a peculiar sensation of satisfaction and fear. She'd noticed the van arrive this morning. She had happened to glance out of her bedroom window while waiting for Tiana to come out of the shower. Alice remembered a van from before . . . three years ago a van had parked for days on end outside their old house while Dax was home, awaiting his placement at the new COLA college up north.

It later turned out there was a surveillance team inside, watching their house. Something about the tinted windows of the BT van along the road had reminded her—and ever since meeting Caroline she had been on edge; expecting something. She had watched the van through a gap in the blinds for another twenty minutes while Tiana had taken ages in the shower . . . but saw nobody either enter or leave it.

And now the van had moved for the first time in nearly three hours—*just* as a girl who looked like Alice Jones, carrying Alice Jones's switched-on mobile phone, had walked past. Coincidentally right after that phone call with Jennifer from COLA Project Control.

Alice knew she didn't have long to make a decision. If they were following Tiana she might have ten minutes, maybe less, before they worked out it wasn't her. Tiana would arrive at home by then and they'd look up who lived there and maybe work out that Tiana looked a lot like Alice and . . .

Anyway. Was she going to sit here and wait to find out how good they were at their job? Or was she going to get out of here while she could? Alice grabbed her mother's grey denim backpack which she had hidden under her bed. She'd taken it when Mum wasn't looking because all her own bags were bright pink or purple and easy to spot. She changed into black jeans and a black shirt which Mum had bought her for a school show she was in; she'd never normally have black in her wardrobe.

She didn't possess a black hat, but had also liberated Mum's God-awful navy beanie from the hatstand. She quickly tucked her long hair up into it and looked in the mirror. She looked like a cat burglar. She threw a blue denim jacket on over the black gear, so she wouldn't look too weird on the street. If she thought she was being followed she could ditch the jacket and change it for the pale green one rolled up in the backpack.

When she had made these preparations on the day she'd come home after meeting Caroline, she had been full of fizzy panic about what might happen if her letter to Dax was intercepted. Making these quick getaway arrangements had been something to do—something which helped her relax. She hadn't *seriously* believed she would ever need them. And as the days had passed she began to think it was all just silliness. Nothing would happen. She was sure of it. Until the van showed up.

OK. She sat down on her bed and caught her breath. There was still a chance she was imagining things. Most likely this was just her being a drama queen and the white van was just a white van . . . and the fact that it had pulled away after Tiana had passed with her friend's mobile signal blinking away in her bag *was* coincidence.

So . . . find out. She called a quick 'I'm going round Tiana's' to her mum as she left the house. But outside she doubled back in the other direction and broke into a run. She could cut across some parkland behind their house and reach Tiana's road from the other end. She could peer along the road, screened by parked cars, and see if the van was anywhere near the house. If it wasn't she could just knock on the door and ask for her phone back and stop being such a nervous wreck.

She ran hard across the park, the backpack of emergency escape supplies whacking up and down on her shoulders. It took five minutes to run to the far end of Tiana's road and another two to creep along it under cover of parked cars until she reached the bend in the road which gave her a view of Tiana's house. She took a moment and readied herself to peel off the stupid beanie hat and run over to get her phone back.

But the hat stayed on. She felt prickles of cold sweat through the black shirt. Parked just one house along from Tiana's was the white BT van. The very same. Same registration number; she'd memorized it. The windscreen was silvery dark. Since when did telephone engineers have tinted windscreens? Her legs felt weak and she crouched down behind a Mercedes 4 x 4 and took long, slow breaths. Then she rose again, turning, and sauntered back the way she'd come. Her legs were still shaking when she reached the park. She kept walking, down to the payphone on King's Way. In her head she recited the number Caroline had written on a slip of paper minutes after she'd bought a cheap new pay-as-you-go phone at the shopping centre.

It had been their last exchange five days go.

'I won't use it for anything,' Caroline had said, switching on the cheap handset and watching its small screen light up blue. 'I won't make a single call—except to you if there's a need. But there won't be. I think you've done your bit, Alice. I don't want you to do anything else.'

'That is a rubbish phone,' Alice had said.

'Yup,' Caroline had grinned back at her. 'But it'll do. And nobody will be tracking it because it's not even registered in my name on the network yet.' She scribbled down the new number. 'Memorize it and then rip this up and bin it on the way home,' she instructed. 'It's a batphone. A hotline from you to me. Nobody else has this number so I will know it's you, wherever you're calling from. And make sure it's a payphone, OK? Not your landline or your mobile. In fact . . . maybe you should keep your mobile off . . .'

'It *is* off,' said Alice. 'Right now. I'm not stupid!'

'Can it stay off?'

Alice gave her a look. 'My LIFE is on my phone!'

But she'd kept it off until she was back at home and trying to be normal again. If she hadn't been seen checking messages every five minutes Mum would have called the doctor.

She slid inside the phone box outside the local newsagents, hoping nobody would notice her. The phone was a clunky grey thing with metal push buttons and a slot for coins or cards. She fed coins into it and dialled the batphone number with shaking fingers. After the fifth ring, Caroline answered. She sounded as if she was outside somewhere.

'What's up?'

Alice swallowed. 'I—er—I think I'm being watched.'

'So what's *new*?'

'No . . . I mean actually watched—by people in a van. I just tricked them. I sent my friend home with my phone in her bag . . . and this van followed her as she went.'

'Are you sure?'

'Yes. I ran around to her road and saw it again—parked just along from her house. Same number plate. Tinted windows.' She could hear the panic making her voice go higher. 'And we got a call from the COLA Project Liaison Officer this morning. Dax has escaped! And they know I've been writing to him. She asked me what I knew.'

'OK . . . take a breath,' said Caroline. 'Where are you now?'

'In a payphone . . . about fifteen minutes from my house.'

'You're probably safe enough,' said Caroline. 'They probably won't come after you. They're just watching in case Dax shows up.'

'But what if they go in and talk to Tiana? What if they find out I planted my phone? They'll know I know about them and . . .'

'Alice—listen. You have two options. You can go home now and act normal. Tell them she took your phone by mistake. Play it dumb—you're good at that.'

'*Thanks*,' muttered Alice. 'And option two?'

'You can run. I have somewhere you can go.'

Alice said nothing, weighing up her choices.

'I think option one is probably OK,' said Caroline. 'If you can tough it out.'

'But what if they get one of their psychics on my case?'

A pause from the other end this time. And then 'Alice—what do you want to do?'

'I want this not to be happening,' said Alice, her voice small and scared. 'But I'm ready to run. I'm not going back there now.'

'Have you got money?'

'Yes. I stole some from Mum's secret stash. She keeps a load of cash in a fake Bible on her bookshelf.'

'OK,' said Caroline. 'Here's where you go. Memorize this address and get yourself there. You'll need to get a bus to the station and catch a train. No taxis. You'll have to walk the last bit. Keep away from security cameras.'

She rattled off an address and Alice repeated it in her head. 'I may not be there when you arrive but don't worry—just nip into the cafe over the road and get something to eat or drink until I get there. With luck, today I'll meet up with Dax.'

'Have you heard from him?' breathed Alice.

'No—but if he got your message he'll know where to find me. Take care, Alice. I'll see you soon.' She rang off.

Alice put the clunky phone back onto its cradle, still repeating the address in her head. She thought she might be sick or wet herself with fear. What the hell was she thinking of? But then she remembered some of the things Dax had told her in their very few days together over the past two years. The things they had done . . . drugging COLAs, putting chips in their heads and tracking them. Other experiments too. And *that* was when Dax still trusted some of them. She shivered, took a deep breath, pulled the beanie hat down over her forehead, and stepped out towards the nearest bus stop.

2 4

The bumpy ride across the Welsh mountains interrupted his reverie. He was losing energy again and would need to take a meal soon. He knew he was faster than a normal peregrine—and any normal peregrine was stupefyingly fast. It was good to be faster—but it meant his energy reserves burned quickly.

He dropped low towards a cluster of peaks he recognized as the Brecon Beacons. There were many travellers out on the roads on this summer's day; tourists taking in the breathtaking views. Dax angled his tail like a rudder and soared away to the greyer, wilder, trackless areas, in search of prey.

A buzzard turned lazily in the sky above him, perhaps eyeing the smaller falcon up as a meal for itself. But it was big and slow—a jumbo passenger plane to his military jet. No threat. Scanning the crags and hills he spotted movement and dropped into a stoop, seizing and killing the young lapwing before it knew anything. His beak snagged the spinal cord through the bird's shimmering green neck feathers, ending its life in a microsecond, and then the pair of them were tumbling to the ground and he was mantling his kill with his wings.

He tried to switch off the boy inside him as he defeathered the warm body and tore at its flesh. If he allowed himself to think as a human, all kinds of unwelcome ideas could come. If he found it this easy to kill an animal . . . how easy would he find it to kill a human? With hot fresh blood on his beak he could not help thinking of Forrester and how easy it might be to end the man.

Of course it might *not* be easy at all. Forrester was tall and lean and probably as fit as the soldiers he commanded. A young dog-fox was hardly a match for that . . . except . . . except for some time now Dax was realizing that he might be more than this. His peregrine form was faster than any other and he had been in a few fights now with the resident foxes in the woods of Fenton Lodge. Dog-foxes could be territorial and he had annoyed more than one. The fights had been swift, visceral, bloody—and he had won every one without trouble; leaving the loser slinking away. None of the foxes he fought had ever returned for a second round.

COLAs were made of tough stuff. This had been proven time and again. They recovered quickly from injury and held their nerve in terrifying situations. He was strong. He was ruthless. He was . . . he *could* be . . . a killer.

And what then? What if he flew back to the lodge, in through Forrester's window, roosted high above the camera in the corner and then shifted and attacked as a fox or an otter before the man knew what had hit him. He could rip his throat out. His jaws were strong in either form but more than that, his determination was fuelled by hatred. He hated that man. He pictured Forrester splayed backwards across his desk—*Chambers's* desk—torn flesh bubbling with choking crimson blood, hands flailing weakly in the air, gurgling for help, eyes wide and panicked and then slowly rolling up; dilated, still . . . empty of life.

For a moment, Dax shifted back to boy form, crouched naked over the shredded body of the lapwing. His skin was instantly chilled as the mountain breeze assailed him. *What are you thinking*? he asked himself. *Who the hell are you any more*?

He let the air cool those maniacal thoughts for a few seconds and then, remembering that people carried binoculars in these parts, shuddered back into feather and took off. He could see nobody for miles but he knew he had been foolish. It was time to focus. Exmoor was probably only thirty minutes away now.

He flew direct; a W-shaped missile cutting through the sky. The mountains fell away to foothills and soon the city of Cardiff bloomed below him in grey and white; and then he was over the Bristol Channel, a wide blue expanse veined by the silty brown of its shallows. The old road bridge flung iron arms up to him and then the new crossing flickered past like a cat's cradle and he flew on, over coast again, feeling the warmth of the land lift him. Now he was minutes away. The rough crags of the North Devon coast softened into pale green and ochre moorland, rising and dipping and pocked with rocky tors. He saw the pattern of the roads and the tree-lined river valleys. He tightened his wide view into binocular precision and found the road leading to the valley which contained the lane which wound down to . . . and there it was. The Owl Box. A small square of grey thatch. He hadn't been here for three years but he knew it instantly. Only something was different. There was a flash of brightness—a rectangle of white—on the roof. He scanned the land around, seeking clues. Were COLA Project spies already here? He could see no sign. Maybe they had been clever and sent just one SAS guy to take him down; someone with the sense to attack via the woods, with stealth and training.

Well, it made no difference; he wasn't landing. Although even up here he could be taken out by a sniper at any moment. He focused on the white rectangle and saw that it was a piece of card, wrapped in plastic. With three words on it. He recognized the writing; it was the same as in her letters. Caroline Fisher had left a note. Was it for him? Of course it was—who else would be reading her note from the sky?

And who else would have any idea what it meant?

WHERE YOU CRIED

Dax flew on south.

25

The place was a ruin. Dax could still recognize it from the foundations and broken walls but barely anything was standing. He shivered as he rode the breeze along the rugged black coast. Below him had once been a state-of-the-art college. Tregarren. The first home of the first COLAs to be found. It was years since he'd been here. In fact the last time he'd seen it, kids were still being stretchered out.

Back then he had only just learned to fly. His new shapeshift had arrived in the nick of time—without it he would never have been able to warn the staff and more than one hundred young COLAs that a tidal wave was about to hit.

He hadn't worked alone that night—Luke had held back that massive wall of water just long enough to save them all—before being swept away himself. That he was back in their lives today, scarred inside but whole outside, was another small miracle of COLA strength.

Where was he now, though? And where was Gideon? Dax felt that familiar boiling of anger and fear inside him as he circled high above the churning Cornish sea. Debris from the tidal wave lay everywhere below him, but one or two buildings were still intact. These were cottages built deep into the cliff above the flat rock promontory where the main campus had been. And an old round engine house, complete with a chimney, still stood at the top of the cliff. Now boarded up and derelict, it had once served as the gatehouse to Tregarren College.

Did he dare fly lower? Could there be someone watching him? Someone hostile? If so, there was no flicker of life he could detect. He coasted down and scanned the windows of the cliffside cottages. Nothing. No movement at all. Had he got it wrong? Misunderstood the message?

Where you cried.

He had cried here. When the college still stood, in his first year. Dax Jones was not one for crying and he hadn't shed a tear for as long as he could remember. He stored every small particle of grief inside himself.

Five years ago he had saved Caroline Fisher's life. She had been about to drown in one of the treacherous bogs that lurked in the moorland of this remote bit of coast. She'd been deliberately misguided off the path; hypnotized. He had saved her—with help from Lisa, Gideon, and Mia, of course. It was the beginning of a bond between them which had been unimaginable when she had first shown up on his doorstep back at his old home with Gina and Alice—a nosy, pushy reporter.

Caroline's suspicion about the freak of nature he had become was confirmed as she lay, crushed and sinking, moments from inhaling mud. He'd had to shift in front of her to save her. That had been quite a day. Minutes after saving her, he was being held at gunpoint and very nearly got killed before witnessing the death of his college principal. So not long after, Dax finally gave in to something he should have done plenty of in his short, unhappy life.

He cried his eyes out.

Caroline had been in a medical wing bed just a few steps away. He hadn't cared. She'd seen it or heard it and later learned, from his letters, that Dax Jones didn't normally cry. Ever. Through those letters—careful and wary at first (they'd been bitter enemies, after all), a friendship and trust had built up. She had given him the key to her cottage; a hideaway in case he ever needed it. This was back in the early days, when the COLA Project did not routinely intercept and read all their private mail. He smiled inwardly as he remembered those times, with Gideon, Lisa, and Mia—all their adolescent issues twisted up with how to manage being a COLA. And there was Owen too—Dax's teacher and friend and foe and hunter and saviour . . . and a heartbreak that nearly shattered him.

So much of his early history lay in the ruins below. But was Caroline Fisher down there somewhere? No. Unless she was hiding deep in one of the cliff cottages, no. And he did not feel at all happy about flying right down and checking through a window. It was too close.

Dax turned in the air, frustrated. His eye was caught by movement back on the land above the cliffs. A motorcyclist was speeding along the B road towards the nearby village of Polgammon. Wearing black leathers and a full-face black helmet. The biker leant low towards the road surface as he or she turned a bend and Dax caught a flash of white on the top of the helmet.

Another flash of white. Also rectangular. Could this be . . . ?

He banked in across the updraft from the cliffside and coasted over the green woods towards the biker. He was just seeing patterns now. It would be nothing. His eye had been caught by similar images since Exmoor. The tops of glasshouses and passing white vans had drawn his eye repeatedly.

But the biker slowed down and turned a circle on the empty road beneath him, resting booted feet on the tarmac. The biker looked up. The biker pointed to the white rectangle and then set off again.

Dax dropped low and read the lettering—astonished.

FOLLOW ME

2 6

Eventually the motorcyclist pulled off the B road onto a farm track and after a couple of minutes bumpy riding, came to a halt beneath some trees. Taking off the helmet, Caroline Fisher shook her hair back and grinned up into the branches. The peregrine falcon was roosting above her.

'Well?' she said. 'Are you going to stay up there all day?'

Dax dropped to the floor and paused. If he shifted back now she would get the full birthday suit experience. He flew into a clump of bushes, shifted, and got up carefully, keeping his lower half modestly shielded by leaves.

'Well, Dax Jones! What a fine figure of a man you've become!' said Caroline and then laughed for quite a while. 'I forgot about the chipped clothes!' she said. She laughed more and wiped tears away from her eyes.

Dax folded his arms across his naked chest and gave her a look. '*Really*?' he said.

'Sorry,' she said, her giggles subsiding. 'I'm a bit hysterical. It's been a weird few days. Dear God, I thought you were *never* coming. If I never sit in another tree with a pair of binoculars again it'll be too soon. If I'd known how long you'd take I could have gone off to the shops and bought some clothes for you.'

'I'll get some,' said Dax. 'I just haven't had time yet. How long have you been waiting here?'

'Oh, only three days,' said Caroline.

He grinned at her. 'Thanks.'

'Are you OK?' she asked. 'Alice showed me your letter. We read between the lines.'

Dax shook his head, still amazed.

'Yeah—who knew? Alice!' said Caroline. 'She's growing up pretty smart. But anyway—what's happening with you?'

'I'm OK,' said Dax, although he suddenly felt so tired he could drop into the bushes and sleep for a day. 'It's the others. Gideon and Luke and all the Cat. As have been taken away. I have no idea where.'

'Cat. As?' asked Caroline, looking puzzled.

'They categorized us all,' said Dax. 'After Chambers left and Forrester came in.'

'Chambers left?' echoed Caroline. 'Where did he go?'

'Look—I've got a lot to tell you,' said Dax. 'I'd prefer to do it *not* standing naked in a patch of holly.'

'I get that,' said Caroline, smiling. 'OK—here's where we're meeting. She rattled off an address. 'It's my friend's place. A holiday home on the Camel estuary.'

'Are you sure it's safe?' he asked. 'There's a good chance they're tracking you. If they send a chopper over The Owl Box and see the sign they'll probably guess you're helping me. I'm sorry—I couldn't risk landing and destroying it.'

'I don't think they're on to me yet,' she said. 'I kind of went dark a few days back. No mobile. No online activity. Left my car well hidden. I think we're OK for now.'

'And Alice . . . wait. Did you say this place is where *we* are meeting? Someone else? You surely don't mean—'

'Yup,' said Caroline. 'If we hurry we might get there half an hour before she does.'

'You're telling me Alice is out there—running to this secure location? *Alice?*' Dax was flabbergasted. It was like hearing a hamster was driving your bus.

Caroline put her helmet back on and clipped the chinstrap. 'Come on—let's get going. I'll race you. And then you can find out for yourself how little Alice has grown up . . .'

The journey took another hour. He could have covered it in ten minutes but he chose to keep Caroline in sight rather than navigate his own direct route. Up here he might be able to spot a car following her. He didn't. And by the time he arrived at the small waterside dwelling, he was as convinced as he could be that nobody was tailing her. He wished he could be more certain about Alice. She was just a kid! But then . . . *he'd* been on plenty of dangerous adventures by the time he was her age. It helped to have superpowers, mind.

The holiday home was made of timber, painted white, with a slate-tiled roof. It was fitted out in a clean, modern style inside, wood walls painted white, rafters painted blue, oak flooring, and minimalist furniture. It wasn't as cosy as The Owl Box but the patio doors at the back gave on to the estuary and the view made up for a lot. Outside was a wooden deck with steps leading down to a small boathouse.

Caroline found a bathrobe for him to wear while he told her about the events of the past few days. She made coffee, and beans on toast as he talked about the changes at Fenton Lodge.

'So . . . Chambers disappears and this new guy comes in and suddenly everything goes off the scale on the security front,' said Caroline, cradling a warm mug in her hands as she settled back into a yellow leather seat, across from the white leather sofa Dax was curled up on. 'What about your college principal—Pauline Sartre? Doesn't she get some say in all this?'

'She went off on compassionate leave about two weeks before it all started,' said Dax. 'Her father died. At least . . . that's what they told us.'

'So,' Caroline pondered, tapping her fingernails against the china mug. 'Who's really behind all this? Not Chambers. He would never approve of this. I've met him. He's devoted to you lot.'

'Before he left he was talking about the new Prime Minister,' said Dax. 'Chambers was expecting a rough patch while the new guy settled in.'

'Hmmm,' said Caroline. 'It's starting to make sense. I wouldn't trust Jonathan Wheeler as far as I could throw him. He's utterly self-serving. I can't believe the British public voted him in. He's not a nice man. So . . . he comes into office and learns about the COLA Project. It scares the pants off him and his first instinct is probably to shut the whole thing down. But that's not an easy thing to do with so many people on the outside connected to it. Think of it . . . the families of more than one hundred kids . . . the staff . . . the military protecting it. It must run to a thousand people. Too many.'

'So—what does he do?' prompted Dax, enjoying the beans on toast immensely. It was his first human meal in a while. It was nice to eat something which he hadn't just slain.

'He gets advised. He gets told about what these kids can do *for* the country. Reminded of what an asset they are. And he doesn't want to lose that BUT he won't risk any one of them getting too much freedom. He wants to keep the power. So—divide and conquer! You take the thing you fear and you cut it into smaller and more manageable pieces. Categorize everyone. Of course. And then get the mind readers out of the way first so they can't tip off the rest of you. If Lisa had picked up anything she'd have told you, yes?'

'I think so,' said Dax. A fleeting memory of her kiss warmed his cheeks a little. 'She was tired and crabby on that last day but she didn't seem to be worried.'

'Well—I bet nobody on site actually knew anything about what was coming,' said Caroline. 'Nothing to read. Nobody but Forrester knew the full plan—and he probably stayed away from you all most of the time.'

'He did,' confirmed Dax. 'He helicopters in from London.'

'Also—these top ex-military operative types have amazing mental discipline,' said Caroline. 'I bet his shutters are well and truly locked in place. Lisa could get past them if she tried, but . . .'

' . . . Lisa never tries,' concluded Dax with a sigh.

'So—like I said—take the psychics away first and then, who next? You Cat. Bs are quite manageable, so you can stay put. The Cat. As, though—big risk. So . . . they have to be taken fast. And the two strongest— Gideon and Luke—got out of the way by deception even before that point. I'm guessing they're housing the Cat. As somewhere super secure. Underground probably.'

'I can't believe they could keep Luke and Gideon in,' said Dax. 'Those two are so strong together—nobody could force them!'

Caroline put down her mug and leaned forward in her seat. 'Dax—they won't use force.' She smiled, sadly. 'They'll use love.'

'What?' Dax shook his head.

'They'll just threaten the people they love. Their dad. Lisa. You.'

Dax swallowed his mouthful of toast and beans and said nothing. Of course. That's exactly what Forrester had done to him—made thinly-veiled threats against his friends if he should ever go AWOL. If he hadn't already taken Gideon and Lisa away, Dax would still be at Fenton Lodge now—caged and angry but trapped . . . by love.

Well that, at least, was a mistake. With the divide and conquer plan, Forrester had taken away his own leverage.

'Well,' said Dax, as something darkened in his heart. 'We have to think of something. We're going to need bigger guns than theirs.'

There was a tap at the door and he and Caroline jumped. She warily crept along the side of the room and Dax instinctively shifted to falcon and flew up to the rafters, out of sight.

The letterbox flapped. 'Caroline?' hissed a high voice.

Relieved, Caroline opened the door and Alice tumbled in like water from a dam. 'Oh thank God!' she said. 'I am SO wrecked!'

Caroline grinned at her. 'Loving the cat burglar look!'

Dax stared down in awe at his little sister, who seemed to have grown a foot taller since he'd last seen her.

'Black!' said Alice, with a shudder, pulling off the beanie hat and letting her hair cascade down her shoulders. 'Ugh! SO depressing! But I knew they'd be looking out for pink. Where's Dax? Have you heard from OW?!!'

Dax couldn't help himself; he'd flown down and landed on her shoulder. His talons had pierced the thin black material of her T-shirt. He hopped across to perch on the back of the sofa while Alice turned and marvelled at him. She hadn't seen him shapeshift very often.

'Dax! You're here! You made it!' She beamed and added, 'Look—I can't give you a hug when you're like that!'

Dax shifted to boy and gave his little sister a big hug. 'Wow, Alice—I am . . . amazed. I never expected you to show up.'

'Well, *thanks*,' she said, sulkily, but she hugged him back. 'Anyway, I didn't have any choice—your COLA guys are after me.'

'They're not *my* COLA guys,' said Dax. 'Not any more.'

Caroline made more beans on toast and Alice sat down to tell Dax about her recent adventures. 'Nice moves!' Dax said, when he heard about her decoy phone deception with Tiana.

'But I was SO scared,' Alice confessed. 'I'm not like you. I don't *do* this kind of thing. I stay at home and watch *Celebrity Cellmates* or go out and buy shiny stuff.'

'Sorry to disappoint you but clearly you're a *lot* like me,' said Dax. 'Minus the feathers, fangs, and fur, obviously. I can't believe you packed an escape bag. That's just what I would do.'

'Yeah . . .' Alice said. 'But you probably didn't put some OPI Red Hot Rio in too.' She dug into the backpack and fished out a little bottle of scarlet nail polish which she waved proudly.

'It's not really my colour,' said Dax.

'Should we let your mum know you're safe?' wondered Caroline.

'How?' said Dax. 'The phones will be tapped—and all Gina's email and social media feeds. I can't think of any way of letting her know. Fly over and drop a message down the chimney or something?'

'Forget it, Dax,' said Caroline. 'They'll be all over the place, watching. You'll be shot out of the sky.'

'I'm more worried about Dad,' said Dax. 'I don't really care about Gina. Sorry, Alice,' he added.

'Don't worry about it,' said Alice. 'She hates you too.'

'Well, nipping up to a North Sea oil rig isn't really on the cards either, right now,' said Caroline.

Dax nodded. In any case, he had another journey in mind. He sat back in the chair and let Caroline fill Alice in on what had been happening to the COLAs. At the end of the story Alice huddled into the sofa, looking forlorn. 'I *love* Lisa,' she said. 'She's got such cool clothes. What are we going to do? How are we going to rescue them?'

There was a long silence. Dax looked at Caroline, wondering if she had come up with a plan. She looked at him, wondering the same.

'Sorry, Dax,' she said. 'I need more time to think. When I set out on this daft mission it was just about you. I didn't think it would be this complicated; this . . . massive.'

'It is massive,' agreed Dax. 'And we need bigger guns.'

'You said that before,' said Caroline. 'But I don't really know what you mean. The big guns are Gideon and Luke—and we can't even find them. If we could just get Lisa out I'm sure she could dowse for them.'

'There *are* bigger guns,' said Dax. 'You know who I mean.'

Caroline blinked. She'd had letters from Dax. Not many—a couple a year—but she knew that he had lost someone he loved. To another country; another dimension almost. She knew that there had been a big catastrophe and it had cost Dax and his friends very dearly.

'Are you talking about Mia?' said Caroline.

Dax nodded.

'But—she's gone. You said so in your letters. Along with that boy—Spook—that you hated. What even happened there?'

'I didn't hate Spook,' said Dax. 'It was more complicated than that. Maybe I hate him now. Mia might still be with us if it hadn't been for Spook. He tricked her—manipulated her; made her go crazy and . . .'

'Sounds like she kind of burnt her bridges at COLA Club,' said Caroline. 'And a lot else besides. But Dax . . . you must have known that sooner or later one of you would go too far.'

'I just never expected it to be Mia,' said Dax, shaking his head. 'Now the COLA Project guys think she's public enemy number one . . . but she isn't. Not really.'

'Mia was lovely,' said Alice. 'I remember her. Even *Mum* liked her . . . before she found out what a bunch of weirdos you all are.'

'Well . . . lovely or deadly—it doesn't really matter either way, does it?' said Caroline. 'Because we have no idea where she is or how to contact her.'

'She's with Spook somewhere,' said Dax. 'There's this boy with them called Olu. He's another COLA but the Project never found him. He can teleport—himself and other people. So they could be anywhere on the planet. Literally.'

Caroline's mouth fell open. 'A teleporter?!' Dax nodded. She blew out a long breath. 'I didn't see *that* coming.'

'You won't see Olu coming either,' said Dax. 'If you don't want to teleported you'd better buy yourself a magnetite necklace. It's the only thing that can stop him. All the COLAs have had magnetite put under their skin.'

Caroline and Alice exchanged amazed glances. 'This is such a brain warp,' muttered Alice.

Caroline blinked a few times and took a breath. 'So— how on Earth do you expect to find Mia?'

'Not a clue. They might not even be on this *planet* for all I know. But . . . there's just one way we might get a message to them.'

Caroline stared at him for a moment. 'Are you serious? I mean . . . yeah . . . bigger guns. But these guys sound like nuclear weapons.'

'And one of them is Mia,' said Dax. 'She's *still* Mia. She still cares about us and she'd go crazy if she knew Lisa and Gideon and Luke were trapped.'

'OK—but we still have the same communication problem,' said Caroline. 'How do we fix that?'

Dax grinned. 'By magic.'

27

The man at the door rubbed his stubbly chin and said: 'Mate—we don't usually deal in cash. You book your ad on the website and pay online.'

Dax nodded. 'I know. And I would. But my parents won't let me have a bank account until I'm sixteen. All I've got is my birthday money in cash—it's the right amount. I just want to place an ad on the website.'

The man looked over his shoulder back into the house and then back at Dax. 'What's your act?'

'Close-up magic,' said Dax. 'But I have a whole new gig planned—I just need to set it up and that's why I have to get an ad in as soon as possible. There's a competition in six weeks—I have to find the right partner and be ready. My act will blow everyone's mind!' He affected a self-impressed expression—just like Spook always used to wear—and handed the piece of paper and the envelope of cash to the man at the door.

This whole thing would have been a lot easier if the offices of *Magicseen* magazine had been anything like he'd imagined. He'd assumed there would be a big shiny window display of previous issues and a door with a bell and someone sitting at a desk, taking calls and emails . . . and cash from teenagers who wanted to place an ad.

He hadn't expected the whole outfit to be run from someone's *house*. Still—at least he hadn't needed to travel too far. The house was in Exeter—just a twenty minute flight from the holiday home on the estuary. It had taken longer for Caroline to nip out and buy him some jeans, a T-shirt, some underwear, socks, and trainers. Showing up naked would definitely have blown his chances of a cash deal.

'OK—look—it's not what we normally do,' said the editor of *Magicseen*. 'But I can see you're in need. I'll check the money and the wording and come back out. Wait here.'

Dax sat on the front lawn and waited. He wondered what the guy would make of the advert he wanted to place.

THE INCREDIBLE FOX BOY SEEKS PARTNER FOR AMAZING NEW ACT.

SPOOK AN AUDIENCE WITH STYLE!
MEET ME at www.thecorridorcave.co.uk FOR
MORE INFORMATION
AND DON'T FORGET TO BRING YOUR PASSION
AND FIRE!

The man came out a few minutes later with a notebook and pen. 'You're on,' he said. 'The ad will be up in the next couple of hours. Good timing, too—because the new online edition goes out this afternoon. We'll be emailing the link to all the subscribers. Your ad should get a lot of attention. I'll need a name and address to go with it. Not for the website; just for our accounts.'

Dax fed him a fake name and address—and a fake mobile number for luck. 'Thanks!' he said. 'I really appreciate it.'

'Sounds like an interesting act,' said the editor. 'Do you dress up as a fox?'

'Kind of,' grinned Dax.

He found a secluded patch of woodland, shifted, and flew back to Caroline and Alice.

'How did it go?' asked Caroline. 'Will one be enough? Should you go for another magazine website too?'

'*Genii* would be good,' said Dax. 'He loves that one too. But I don't think I've got time to fly to Washington DC with a beak full of dollars. And we can't pay online because . . .'

'Yeah,' said Caroline. They'd already had this discussion. Any form of online payment would leave a hot trail to where they were. Caroline had money in her bank account and on credit cards—but no way of using it and staying under the COLA Project radar. Alice had a bank account too—but the problem was the same. How they would manage for food was going to crop up soon. A lot of Caroline's ready cash had been used up buying him clothes. Dax didn't like to thieve but he suspected his shapeshifting would be put to criminal use soon. He guessed he would have no choice.

'How do we know this Spike guy will see it?' asked Alice.

'Spook,' corrected Dax. 'And we don't . . . but I bet he will. He's a person of habit. He loves his magic magazines and he never misses an issue. He was always reading them when he was at Fenton Lodge; always ordering new tricks and DVDs from them. We weren't allowed to have the Internet, so he couldn't check things out online—but I bet he does now. He'll want to read all the new stuff the minute it's published, so he'll subscribe to the online editions too. I'm sure of it.'

'But why does he even need that stuff?' asked Alice. 'He's a COLA, isn't he? He can do illusions dead easy!'

Dax nodded. 'True—he doesn't need trickery; he's the real deal. But he wanted to learn to be a normal magician. He wanted to be famous. He's got an ego the size of Jupiter anyway, and he could see how it could be a career for him in the real world. He'd be kind of hiding in plain sight, pretending all his illusions were just clever tricks from a brilliant young magician, when they were actually something way more impressive—and scary. So he learned to do all the card trick stuff—all that really impressive shuffling and flipping and sleight of hand. He's good. I hate to admit it, because he's also a total arse. But he's good.'

'OK—so let's say he picks up your message,' said Caroline. 'Do you really think he'll travel all the way to some cave in the middle of the Scottish Highlands to talk to you? He can't stand you!'

'You're right. He can't stand me. But . . . we have a past. Something I can't really explain happened in that cave and if Spook hadn't been there to help me a lot of us—maybe all of us—would be dead.' Dax wrinkled his brow under his dark fringe, remembering. It was hard to imagine he and Spook had ever worked together . . . but they had. 'Also,' he added, 'he doesn't have to make a huge journey to get there. With Olu's help he can be on that mountain in seconds. Maybe even *in* the cave. Maybe not, though, because Olu can't teleport anywhere he can't see first. There needs to be a photo or something. And I don't think anyone has ever taken a photo of that place.'

'Well then,' said Caroline. 'You'd better get going. I hope he doesn't show up too soon and not wait. Not everyone's as patient as I am, Dax Jones.'

He grinned. 'I really appreciate it. But with Olu on hand, if I'm not there Spook can check back every ten minutes if he fancies it, from the comfort of his own home or luxury yacht, or wherever he lives these days.'

'Good,' she grunted. 'Because *I* was only going to give it another hour and you'd have been on your own.'

'OK,' said Dax. 'And what will you two do? Just stay here and keep your heads down?'

'For now,' said Caroline. 'Once you're back we can plan what to do next. But Dax . . . if you're bringing big guns back with you, you'd better make sure the safety catches are on.'

28

Dax sailed high through the thin air, surfing the choppy thermals as he searched for the path below. The last time he'd been on this mountain he hadn't paid very close attention to his surroundings. His route had been clearly marked inside his brain by some unfathomable instinct.

And he'd come here with the one COLA he liked least in the world. Spook Williams had been none too keen either, on being compelled to journey into the bowels of the Earth just to hold his enemy's hand—but it *had* been a matter of life and death.

Their alliance had been brief and uncomfortable and since then their instinctive mutual mistrust had reasserted itself. Dax had learned to dislike Spook all over again—and then to hate him when he stole Mia away from the tight-knit group of friends.

So asking for his help was only a matter of desperation. Somehow, Dax had to convince Spook to take him to Mia. Or maybe make a direct appeal to Olu—because Olu would be there. The only way Spook could reach the mountain cave was by travelling with the teleporter.

But what if neither of them were there? What if the illusionist *hadn't* seen the message in *Magicseen*? As he coasted down to the steep mountain path they had travelled more than two years ago, Dax was losing confidence as well as height. What were the odds? Even with an email reminder to the subscribers? He may well have looked through the online magazine, but even so he could have missed the advert. Dax could end up sitting alone in the dark for days.

Dax landed and stared around for the entrance to the cave. At first glance he saw nothing but coarse vegetation and rocky outcrops, but suddenly—there. There it was. Shivering, Dax clambered up to a patch of heather which fell in a springy overhang. How he knew this was the right place, he had no idea. It looked very much the same as countless other clumps of heather he had passed. He pushed at it and saw a familiar dark sliver of space.

The gap was barely wide enough to wriggle through but he managed it. Once over the lip of stone he lurched forward into the blackness and then slid on his belly, slowly at first but then at gathering speed. It was utterly dark. And utterly terrifying. He spun around on the slippery slope, whirling 180 degrees against rock which felt like gently ribbed glass under his palms. He tried vainly to slow his descent. It was like being swallowed. He was shooting feet-first down the mountain's gullet, spiralling around the flume of stone and hardly able to catch a breath. Finally he shot out into a wider space. He put his hands up just before headbutting a wall of granite.

His ragged gasps echoed around the circular chamber. There was a dim light—a pale golden glow from one thin beam which projected at ninety degrees from the centre of the cave floor. The beam hit the cave wall and disappeared through it, as if it had tunnelled a path. As his breathing calmed, Dax could hear a low, sweet note sounding from the beam . . . like a choir singing, a long way distant.

He got to his knees and crawled across to it. The beam was beautiful . . . like liquid gold. Dax tentatively reached towards it and put a finger into its path. Instead of deflecting, the light seemed just to pass through his finger, gold brightness flaring through the skin and silhouetting the bone inside. It felt tingly.

There was a cough. Dax glanced up.

'Have we finished playing with the nice light?' The voice was laconic, drawling, superior. So familiar. So detested and yet so welcome. Cold whiteness suddenly uplit the angular features of Spook Williams's face.

'You got the message!' Dax felt dazed. The plan had worked. It had *worked*.

'Evidently,' said Spook. 'I haven't been hanging around in here for fun, you know. Sorry if we caught you by surprise.'

Dax realized he was lighting his face with the torch app on his mobile phone. It also lit Olu, standing a little way behind him, watching silently.

'You didn't,' said Dax. 'I knew you were here. I could smell the stuff you use on your hair ten minutes before I got here. Oh dear . . . did you headbutt the rock?' He could see a dark smudge on Spook's right cheekbone.

'I did,' said Spook, with a tight smile and a narrowing of his amber eyes. 'Thanks for noticing. Now—I wasn't keen to be here the last time you dragged me into your plans and I've got no great inclination to be here now—'

'So why did you come?' said Dax, cutting through Spook's self-impressed monologue. He was noticing more now—the calf-length black leather coat, the pointed black boots, black jeans, and jade shirt; some kind of silver talisman at the boy's throat, his hair still slicked back into sculpted waves of dark red. Spook had not lost his taste for magician fashion. Or expensive cowhide. All he needed was the little beard . . . but maybe ginger didn't work so well for that.

'I would have ignored your childish message,' said Spook. 'If it were down to me, you'd be rattling around this godforsaken chamber pot on your own time. I don't owe you anything.'

'Don't you?' asked Dax.

There was a thick silence. Eventually it was broken by Olu. 'Can you two get to the bloody point?' he said, in his flat Mancunian twang. 'I'm freezing my butt off down here.'

Dax nodded. 'I need Mia,' he said. 'We all . . . need Mia. Something's happened.'

'Let me guess,' said Spook. He adopted a fake sympathetic pout and the voice to go with it. 'Old Auntie COLA not been playing fair with you? Did she let the nasty man take your friends away?'

Dax blinked. 'You *know*?'

'That you've slowly become slaves to the government?!' Spook gave a hollow laugh. 'I saw that coming *years* ago. I'm just astonished that nobody else did. Mia saw it too—that's why she left.'

Dax gritted his teeth. 'Like she had any choice after what you did!' he bit back.

'Guys, guys . . .' Olu interjected. 'Seriously. I'm going.'

Spook grabbed his arm. 'Wait,' he said. There was acid in his tone and Dax realized very quickly that he and Olu weren't exactly best mates. That gave him some satisfaction. However cool Spook liked to think he was, the teleporter saw through it. Dax found himself grinning at Olu and Olu rolled his eyes. Yep. There it was. Two of them knew what Spook was.

'I've cut out the magnetite,' he said, to Olu, not to Spook. He held up his palm to display the thin red scar where he'd sliced out the mineral lozenge which would have prevented Olu teleporting him. 'Things are bad. Really bad. Jake and Alex say hi, by the way.'

Olu's face lit and clouded in a microsecond. He cared about the Teller brothers. In a way that hurt him. 'They OK?' he asked.

'For now,' said Dax. 'But since I escaped . . . I don't know. Olu—please—take me to Mia. I have to tell her what's going on. We need to work together or our kind will be controlled, imprisoned . . . yes . . . Spook . . . enslaved. Enjoy your moment. You were right.'

Spook smirked. He held fast on to Olu's wrist and nodded towards Dax. 'Go on,' he said.

Olu shook him off. 'I don't need your permission, mate,' he snapped.

He stepped across to Dax and put out his hand. Dax took it and the next thing he knew, he was in Argentina.

29

Alice missed her smartphone. It was less than half a day since she had dumped it in her friend's bag and let it lead the COLA Project snoops off on a wild goose chase. The hours since had been terrifying and exhilarating— the running across the park, calling Caroline from a phone box like a spy, catching the bus, avoiding security cameras, getting the train . . . buying a local map book and then walking from the station to the cottage (no taxi allowed) . . . and then finding Dax waiting for her— proud of her.

She had done the right thing. She'd been . . . well, honestly, she'd been more than a little bit cool.

So although her thumbs twitched to get back online and update her mates with the latest, she grinned to herself. She had dumped the phone. She was tech-free. She was OFF THE GRID. It was exciting to not know what would happen next. Exciting to be a kind of fugitive. Nobody but Dax and Caroline had any idea where she was. Maybe they didn't even know she was missing yet. Maybe they were still camped outside Tiana's house, waiting for her to go back home. Even Mum might not have raised the alarm yet.

She went to lean on the balcony and take in the view.

'Want another cuppa?' Caroline called from the kitchen area.

'Yes please,' called back Alice, watching a small dark motor launch mark a foaming V shape across the estuary.

The small TV in the kitchen burbled away as Caroline got out mugs and filled the kettle. The water lapped gently at the shoreline down by the boathouse and insects droned in the early evening warmth. Alice was calm; serene, almost. It felt good to know you weren't being watched or tracked.

The motor launch did a U-turn, sending surf spraying up in an arc. Alice thought she would like a trip in a motor launch. She liked speed and she liked the water; swimming was the only sport she was good at in school.

The launch was coming back along their side of the estuary. She squinted at it, shielding her eyes from the last slanting rays of the sunset with one hand. Maybe it was a neighbour's boat. Not a very holiday-friendly colour, though—black.

In the house she heard a crash and a moan from Caroline; she must have dropped a mug. 'You need a hand with that?' Alice called back, glancing over her shoulder. There was no reply. The silence was what did it. Instantly Alice's skin was awash with goosebumps. She turned slowly and saw nobody in the cottage. No Caroline; no Dax, getting back early. Nothing. She moved silently along the balcony, towards the steps leading to the boathouse, her breath paused and her heart thudding.

The black motor launch got closer and Alice

realized it didn't look like a holiday boat because it was *not* a holiday boat. It wasn't aiming for a neighbouring boathouse, either. It was heading straight for this one.

Back in the cottage she saw a dark shadow flit along a wall. The thudding of the boat engine grew loud enough to cover her frantic footfalls as she dashed down the steps towards the shore and began to crunch across the shingle. Her first thought was to hide in the boathouse, but the black motor launch would block her exit on to the water. She could run up the side passage to the road—where no doubt an army of COLA Project 4 x 4s would be waiting. Glancing around for any other escape, Alice made a decision. It was something she would never, ever have done if she hadn't just lost her mind. The deck adjoined the property next door. Beneath it was a metre-high space; a kind of tunnel under the decking. It was full of junk and festooned with spider webs. Alice had always been terrified of spiders but there were things in the world, with fewer legs, which she was much more scared of. She ducked under the deck, brushing webs away from her face as she stumbled along, crouched over, picking her way across old crates and oars and deflated dinghies.

Behind her, the motor launch engine cut out and she heard a man's voice through a two-way radio. 'She's running,' it said. 'She won't get far. Keep it quiet. Discreet. Out.'

Alice ran on, glad that huge banks of damp, smelly seaweed were deadening the noise underfoot. *What had they done with Caroline? She hadn't even cried out. Had they just knocked her out cold? Or . . . killed her?* A whimper of fright escaped her and she slapped her hands over her mouth as a cloud of flies rose off the seaweed pile she'd just kicked through. She'd reached the end of the neighbours' crawlspace and now she was faced with some kind of nylon mesh stretched across it, blocking her way. Beyond it was a tiny slant of sun, marking the gap between this house and the next one—and another area of under-deck which might shelter her escape for a few more metres.

With desperation she clawed at the mesh. And a second later, for the first time in her life, Alice was able to claim a useful function for glittery nail varnish. It set like concrete. It was actually hell to get off, even with nail polish remover. And it really strengthened her nails. She had filed them into very good talons and one of these caught at a weak spot in the nylon mesh. The mesh, obviously pretty old and perished, tore right to the ground. Alice shoved through it, now careless of more spider webs across her face, and sped across the sliver of sunlight and into the dark safety of the next boardwalk tunnel.

She paused, trying to calm her rapid breathing and listen. She heard voices a house or two away, from where she'd come. Then she heard a knock. It was the house next door. Frozen with fear, she heard a woman answer the door. 'I'm sorry to bother you, madam,' said a male voice. 'We're trying to find a lost child—holidaymaker—her name's Alice. Here's a recent photo. Have you seen her? We think she may be in this area.'

'Well, I don't know . . .' said the woman, thoughtfully, and Alice did not wait to hear more. She could see another boathouse—a smaller one with an open door—just a short sprint away. She needed to get to it and find a better place to hide or a boat or something. *Oh yeah? You think you're going to row away from that launch, do you?* She ran anyway, keeping low and reaching the doorway in seconds. Inside the wooden shed it was cool and shady with an ever-shifting floor of shallow water. There were two canoes tied up at the side, with paddles above them on hooks. Could she canoe? She'd never tried. And anyway—the canoes were bright orange; not exactly easy to slip away in unnoticed.

She could climb up into the rafters and . . . *Oh who are you kidding?* her mocking inner voice chimed in again. *Like they're not going to search every building along this shore! Give it up, Alice! What are they going to do? Try to get stuff out of you. Well, it doesn't matter now because Dax is free and he's getting help from Mia and . . .*

There was a wetsuit. And a snorkel. Both black; hung up on the opposite wall. Both small. Alice ignored the mocking voice and grabbed them. Maybe she wasn't done just yet. She flung her clothes off and struggled into the wetsuit in her underwear; it was a little baggy but not too bad—a woman's size. She pulled the hood, goggles, and the snorkel on over her hair. Were there flippers? She glanced around. Where? There they were—on a shelf by the canoes. She put them on and was about to get into the water when she saw her clothes lying on the concrete floor. She picked them up and stuffed them deep into one of the canoes. Then she stood for a few seconds, head tilted, listening. She heard a door bang and something that might have been the crackle of a two-way radio. A boat engine purring along—towards her or away? It didn't matter. She had to go. Now.

Careful not to make a loud splash, she slid into the water, gasping at the cold, even in summer, then took a deep breath, pulled the snorkel mouthpiece between her teeth, snapped the goggles across her eyes, and went under.

3 0

The heat and the smell was intense. Dry and aromatic. And the sunlight slanting across the mountain slopes was bright afternoon gold.

'Where are we?' was Dax's first question as soon as he'd got over the nausea and disorientation.

'Mendoza,' said Olu, sitting down on the wooden veranda. 'Vine-growing region of Argentina. How you doin'?'

'OK,' said Dax, getting up off his hands and knees and sitting down heavily next to Olu. He shook his swimming head. 'You do this all the time? Every day?'

'Any time I like,' said Olu, resting his elbows on a higher step and grinning at Dax.

'Where's Spook?' asked Dax.

'Left him behind in the cave of wonders,' said Olu. 'He was annoying me.'

'You don't say.' Dax found himself grinning back at the boy—and then had to stop himself. He didn't want to like Olu. Not after the things Olu had done; the distress he had caused. Last summer he had stolen Jake and Alex Teller away from them all and plunged the brothers into a life and death drama in which they were forced to use their talents for crime—and a bitterly cruel deception. It had come close to ending their lives and it had badly hurt David Chambers.

Dax knew enough about what had happened to realize it wasn't all Olu's doing—but Olu had been a willing enough accomplice. And then he'd helped Spook when Mia was taken from them.

'I'll go back for him in a minute,' Olu added. 'Let him stew a bit.'

Dax glanced around at the building behind them. Nestling into the hillside was a kind of wooden chalet, large and expensively designed, with floor-to-ceiling glass windows offering panoramic views the valley below. The slopes of the valley looked like neatly combed hair, with thin lines of low-growing vines, sweeping as far as the eye could see. The lines followed every rise, fall, and swell of the land like a vast, green-and-gold fingerprint. 'So . . . is Mia here?' he asked.

Olu didn't answer. He didn't need to. Suddenly Dax was filled with a sense of calm, of warmth, of happiness. It struck him in a wave just as the unmistakable scent of her drifted in.

He turned to see her standing in a wide aperture in the glass. She was wearing a long cotton dress, the colour of buttermilk, simple and sleeveless and elegant. Her feet were bare. Her travels had not given her a tan; she was still pearly pale and her eyes were as startlingly violet as he remembered, under a heavy fringe.

'Your hair suits you like that,' was all he could think of to say.

She flicked slender fingers through the choppy cut and smiled. 'I get it done in Paris,' she said. 'You look . . . taller.'

He nodded. What did you say? What did you say to a friend who had left you—to join someone who was your enemy? 'Is it working out?' he said, at length. 'Living with Spook and Olu and . . . your grandfather?'

She shrugged. 'How's COLA Club worked out for *you*?'

Dax opened his mouth and then closed it again. There was too much to say.

'Olu,' said Mia, turning to the teleporter. 'Please go and fetch Spook. You know he'll be in a foul mood for *days* now. We've spoken about this before, haven't we?'

Olu got up with a sigh. 'Oh come on,' he said. 'He's just *asking* to be left helpless in a cave. You know it.'

'Even so,' said Mia, and something in her voice and her eyes, as they glanced across at Olu made Dax shiver. 'Oh—and don't bring him back here immediately. I'd like to have a little catch up with Dax. Give us twenty minutes.'

Olu nodded and disappeared. Dax stared at Mia. 'You're really ruling the roost these days, aren't you?'

She smiled. 'Speaking of the roost—how did you escape from yours? From what I heard, that electromagnetic dome was falcon-proof.'

'You *know* about that?' Dax was astonished.

'We have a very good network of informants,' said Mia, sitting down on the veranda next to him. 'We know

171

pretty much everything. We've seen this day coming for months. So . . . how did you get out?'

Dax had to fight the waves of feel-good she was sending out. It had been nearly a year since he'd seen her—time to lose some of his resistance to the Mia Effect. If he wasn't careful he might just lay his head in her lap and forget the world.

'It *was* falcon-proof,' he said. 'But not human-proof.'

'You mean you vaulted over those four-metre walls on a pole?!' she laughed.

'No. I flew through them. I just shifted at the last moment, enough to get through the boundary without losing consciousness. Then I had to shift back again in time not to hit the ground.'

Mia gaped at him. 'Are you serious?! Dax—that was insane!'

'Yes,' said Dax. 'It was. But Clive helped me to train.'

'Clive!' she smiled again. 'Oh, I have missed Clive.'

'Have you?' Dax heard the coldness creeping into his voice. 'And the rest of us? Maybe you've been having too good a time teleporting around the world to think about what you left behind.'

The smile vanished and for a moment he thought he saw a flash of the old Mia—vulnerable and anxious. Then she took his hand and a huge wave of comfort hit him.

'No!' He pulled away from her and stood, backing along the veranda. 'Stop giving me The Effect,' he said. 'I'm not just anyone, you know, Mia. I know what you can do. I have seen it. I have seen it all. I've seen you save people. And I've seen you kill people.'

She stood up too, but didn't attempt to get closer—or to send any more Effect. She looked down at her bare feet. 'Dax—you have no idea how much I've missed you all. You, Gideon, Luke . . . Lisa.' She gulped. 'Especially Lisa. I'm surrounded by men and boys. I have no best friend to talk to any more.'

'Spook didn't turn out to be good boyfriend material then?'

She caught her breath and shook her head. 'Spook and me . . . it's not something I can explain.'

'So . . . would it have killed you to write?' demanded Dax, aware that he was beginning to sound like her dad.

She lifted her chin. 'What are the odds my letters would have arrived?'

He didn't have an answer for that. He didn't even know what, specifically, he was so angry about. Mia told him.

'You feel deserted. I'm sorry, I can't change that,' she said. 'I *did* desert you all. But, Dax, you know I had no choice.'

He drew a long breath and then he shifted and took a long flight around the valley of vines, allowing the warm air to lift him, zoning out for a few minutes. She stood still on the veranda, her thin cotton dress moving gently in the breeze, watching him with her eyes shielded by one hand. When he landed at her feet and shifted back to boy again, she put her arms around him and held him close, enveloping him in her warmth and love. It was dizzying but he hugged her back for a few moments, sending his own warmth and love.

Eventually they stood apart and she said: 'We don't really have much time, do we? We have to get Lisa, Gideon, and Luke out of their prisons. We have to act soon, before Forrester knows what's happening.'

'So . . . you know about *Forrester* too,' said Dax.

'Come inside, have some food and drink,' said Mia. 'I'll tell you what I know and you can tell me what you know. And then we will make a plan.'

3 1

Alice went with the current. She dived down as low as she could on full lungs and swam where the water took her. How far from the boathouse she was travelling she had no idea, because she didn't dare raise her head from the water. She only allowed the tip of the snorkel to breach the surface when she needed more air. She hoped the water wasn't too clear where she was swimming— it looked pretty dim. The seaweed and the silt she was stirring up might camouflage her. She was glad the wetsuit wasn't bright red or orange like some she'd seen. She tried to swim economically, as she'd been taught. Too much arm and leg flapping would be obvious; she'd leave a wake, even below the water.

She did a gentle front crawl, driving her arms downwards with each stroke and paddling her feet fast and shallow—occasionally pulling herself along against submerged rocks and weed. Fish slipped past her and spiny crabs danced sideways in slanting rays of pale golden-blue; the setting sun's last reach. *Where are you going?* that voice was demanding now. *You have to aim for somewhere! You might be swimming round in circles. You could end up right back where you started!*

She had to think. If she was following the tide, she

would be heading back out to sea, wouldn't she? That probably wasn't the best idea. No, she needed to get out of the water, to somewhere under cover—another boathouse or a wooded creek; or maybe climb up the hull of a moored yacht and see if she could get inside it.

She would have to take a look, to raise her head up and see where she was in relation to the land. But even as she thought this she sensed the throb of a motor in the water, nearby. Was it the black launch? Were they following her?

It could be any launch. She had no idea. She was pretty much swimming blind. What seemed like a good idea at the time now seemed idiotic. Exhaustion was beginning to get a hold. She had never trained for long distance swimming. Her arms and legs were aching and her head was feeling weirdly hot. What if she passed out? Here? Underwater?

The throb of the engine seemed to be getting quieter. She directed herself away from it and made for a shadow above her which looked like the bottom of a small boat. She made a couple of lunges and burst through the water to one side of it—hoping she had chosen the right side to shelter her from anyone's view. In the flare of sunset through her dripping goggles she thought she'd chosen right. There was a stretch of high reeds off to her left. The boat was a small wooden dinghy, anchored just four or five metres from the shore. It was quiet. She held on to the stern, pulling the snorkel and the goggles onto her forehead, and weighed up whether she had the energy to climb into the vessel and hide. Would that action cause enough movement and noise to give her away to her pursuers?

She was beginning to shiver. *You can't wait*, that voice told her. *You're only going to get colder and this is only going to get harder. Swim into the reeds or get into this boat. Now.*

The reeds would wave violently, like a white flag, if she went into them. No. She would go for the boat. She grasped the stern with one hand, reaching around its wooden flank with the other, and then tried to fling her leg up over one side. The flipper on her foot made this impossible. She reached down and pulled her flippers off, dropping them into the boat before catching her breath and trying again. This time she managed to get her whole knee over.

But she hadn't thought it through. The small boat wasn't stable enough to allow her to crawl up over its edge. It flipped up to meet her and in a microsecond she realized the extent of her mistake. The whole thing was up on end and tipping over on top of her. It thudded brutally down across her brow and slapped her back into the water. She went under, seeing blotchy blue stars. She tried to grasp the upturned boat, to find a hand-hold, a way back up. It flipped again, releasing its store of captured air in a big belch and then slid back onto her face. She had no air! No air! The snorkel was knocked off and the boat was blocking her route to the surface. She had to get out from under it but she didn't know which way to go. Oh God. She needed to breathe. She needed to breathe. She was going to breathe. She was going to breathe in water . . .

Bubbles escaped her, tickling past her face and vanishing into the shadow of the upturned boat. Her last gasp . . . there it went. It was all over. Her stupid, dizzy adventure . . . was all over.

There was a flash of light. A sudden churning. Was this the way it finished? Bright light?

She was seized and dragged to the surface where she was suddenly dragging in air and pushing out water with harsh barks and growls, like a rabid dog in its death throes. She passed out for a few seconds and then she was lying on her side in a pool of water and vomit and a man was slapping her cheek and saying 'Alice? Alice Jones?'

Another man said: 'It's her. Call in to Control.'

3 2

'Gideon and Luke are *here*.' Mia zoomed in on her tablet and showed him a satellite view of some angular concrete structures, surrounded by greenery. 'It's in East Sussex. An old nuclear bunker designed for the country's ruling class, back in the fifties—just in case. It looks derelict at a glance. And until a few months ago it was. Now it's what Category A COLAs will be calling home.'

Dax stared at the image, aghast. 'They're all underground?'

'Yes,' said Mia.

'Where else would they be?' snorted Spook. He was standing behind with Olu, still seething about having been left in the cave on his own for ten minutes. Seconds after their return, Olu gave a cry of horror from the other end of the room where the mirror told him his hair was on fire. Mia hadn't raised her head from the desk where she and Dax had been looking at plans and print outs. She'd merely said: 'Spook—behave.' And Spook had sighed and lifted the illusion.

Then Olu had attempted to port him away somewhere ugly, but Spook now had magnetite in his fist and pressed against his chest—a dark gleaming medallion—and Olu was unable to extricate him.

Now Spook was enjoying his moment of satisfaction over Dax—that his predictions had come true. 'Did you think they'd put them in a penthouse in the city?' he snickered.

Dax ignored him. 'How did you get this information?' he asked Mia. 'Surely you didn't port into the COLA Project HQ in Whitehall?'

'Not Whitehall, no,' said Mia. 'An admin office round the corner, where Forrester's secretary works. I convinced another employee to take a photo on her phone for me. Showed it to Olu and—in we went.'

Dax nodded. Olu needed to see a place before he could port into it but a photo was good enough. 'And how did you convince this secretary to give up the information?' he asked in a low voice. Did he want to know?

'I took some pain away for her,' said Mia. 'Anyway, that's not important. This is. Olu can't get us inside the bunker. The plans are not available and there are no photographs. These old places were kept very secret; they didn't want all the riffraff banging on the doors as the mushroom cloud went up.'

Dax sighed as he gazed at the image on the screen. It looked like nothing more than a pale C-shaped scar in the land. 'And where is Lisa?' he asked.

'She's in Gloucestershire,' said Mia. She brought up another satellite image—much clearer—of a country estate in rolling green hills—many miles from any town. 'This is easier. You could get in here. Although they'll know you're missing now and will be throwing extra security up everywhere. They might even have another dome set up, although they didn't when we checked. Not as far as we could tell.'

'A dome wouldn't keep me out,' said Dax. 'Getting in from outside a dome is easier—I could go in at the lowest level—the curve is in the easy direction. But if you've checked it out, how come you haven't gone in with Olu?'

'No house plans or photos,' said Mia. 'They've taken care to remove any images of this place, hard copy or online. They're wise to Olu. We could go into the grounds and hopscotch across—but we might still end up stuck outside; the windows are all tinted. You can see out but not in. None of the ground floor windows appear to open and there are restrainers on the upper floor windows. They have trained dogs too, snipers, the lot. The roof was a possibility but it was very risky. We've been working on a different kind of plan anyway. But then Spook found your message. It seemed like the answer had just flown in.' She held up a digital camera. 'All you need to do is find an open window, get in there, take a photo, and get out again.'

Dax glanced back at the screen. 'I can do that here,' he said, nodding at the Gloucestershire estate. 'But here?' He swiped back to the image of the bunker in the trees. 'I can't see any windows—can you?'

Mia shook her head. 'No. No windows. But there are vents. Like chimneys. Several of them. Seventy-eight centimetres in diameter. We think they go down at least thirty metres.'

'You said you haven't got any pictures or plans,' pointed out Dax.

'True,' said Mia. 'But this bunker is like others in design. A load of them were built in the fifties. Some of them have become museums or even private homes and we've taken a look at *their* plans. That's how we've got some idea of what's likely to be down there. So—thirty metres down, seventy-eight centimetres wide. Can you do it?'

Dax stared at the ceiling, calculating the space and the drop. Once he had committed there would be no turning back. There simply wouldn't be space to turn around and he would barely be able to spread his wings.

'That's not all,' said Mia. 'There are fans in the vents. They're for pushing out heat and carbon dioxide—the fresh air goes in through different filters. The cap at the top is easy; you can get that off with a screwdriver—or even your talons. But there are three, maybe four fans at intervals down the pipe.'

Dax shook his head. 'So how do I get past those?!'

'It depends,' said Mia. 'On how fast they're going.'

He stared at her. 'You think I can fly through a turning fan?'

She pulled a large folded piece of paper from the desk. 'This is the model of vent they are using in a bunker in East Anglia. We're pretty sure the vents will be the same design. Some have three fans—some have four, depending on how long they are. The fans turn quite slowly—they're not designed to go at high speed unless there's some kind of emergency. They move steadily—predictably. Think of them as windmill sails.'

Dax twitched visibly and she touched his arm. 'Sorry.'

He shook her off. 'Go on.'

'So what I'm saying is that you can probably drop through if they're going slowly. And they should be.'

'OK—so I get down there and get a photo. Then what? You think I can fly back up that pipe?'

'I don't know. Can you?'

Dax eyed the drawings on the desk. In this bunker—not even necessarily identical to the one they were targeting—the vents ended in the ceilings a good three metres above the floor below. With a horizontal flight across a room or along a length of corridor, building some momentum, he *could* flip up and back into the vent space. Perhaps the rising updraft that turned the fans would help—but he'd be trying to keep momentum and get up through turning fans with wings flapping wildly. He shook his head, thinking hard. He would need to disable the fans on his downward journey.

'How wide is it again?'

'Seventy-eight centimetres across,' said Mia, watching him closely.

He closed his eyes for a few moments, visualizing the descent and the plan which might . . . only *might* . . . work.

He opened his eyes again and nodded. 'I can do it,' he said. 'But even if I get you in . . . this place is vast. And there will be cameras and security guys and God knows what else in place.'

'I didn't say it would be easy,' said Mia. 'It's a risk I'm willing to take.'

And then he remembered what she was. He was a boy who could shapeshift into three forms. All of them pretty low threat. She was a girl would could heal the world—or set it on fire. A category for Mia didn't exist.

'Come on then. Call Olu in. I'll go now,' he said.

'No you won't,' she said.

'Mia—our friends need our help!' he insisted.

'Yes. They do. What they don't need is some botch job,' she said. 'Dax—you're dead on your feet. When did you last sleep? You're not going anywhere until you've had some rest and some food.'

Dax realized she was right. Exhaustion hit him like a lump hammer the second he gave it some thought. He had been on the run for less than twenty-four hours and in that time he had crossed the UK in both directions and then travelled halfway across the planet.

She took his hand and led him to the open tread wooden stairs that angled out from a white marble wall with no visible support. 'Up the top, to the left,' she said. 'It has an en suite. You could use a shower.' she wrinkled her nose slightly. 'You're a bit . . . foxy.'

Dax grinned. Yeah. He stank. He didn't really care.

'Then sleep for a couple of hours. When Olu takes you back it'll be fully dark—the best time to get into the bunker. Do you need help to get to sleep?'

He shook his head. If he let her calm him too much he might go under too far. He wanted sleep but he did not want to lose his wariness. Not with Spook in the building. He found the room—cool and white with a pale wood floor—and showered, relishing the warm running water and citrus-scented gel. Then he crept in under the light white duvet, sank into the pillows, and fell asleep.

When he awoke Mia was standing a short distance away, gazing at him.

'I didn't want to wake you,' she said. 'You looked so peaceful.'

He sat up.

'There's food downstairs,' she said. 'Olu got takeaway. KFC.'

Dax nodded. He could smell it. 'Where did he get KFC from out here?'

'He got it from Leicester Square, London,' said Mia, raising one eyebrow.

Dax chuckled. Of course. Distance was nothing to a teleporter. The fried chicken and chips were still piping hot when he got downstairs. They all ate quickly. Dax drained a large paper beaker of Pepsi too. He was going to need the sugar boost.

When the meal had ended Dax studied the plans one more time, took the small camera from Mia, pushed it deep into his jeans pocket, and reached out a hand to Olu.

'Be careful,' said Mia, touching his face and sending in a wave of warmth. 'Get in—get the photo and get out. Please don't go off on a mission on your own. I don't want to lose you.'

Spook stood behind her, looking brooding. Jealous. Dax gave him a tight smile and a cocky salute before Olu pulled him into another dimension.

33

Alice was reunited with Caroline in an armoured truck. Caroline was cuffed by one wrist to the low metal bench she was sitting on. She looked furious. Alice slumped down opposite in the damp wetsuit, her hair hanging like seaweed across her face, as she too was cuffed.

'You have no right to be doing this,' stated Caroline. 'This is unlawful kidnap!'

One of the men fixed her with a stare as he went to close the back door of the truck. 'Don't be naive, Miss Fisher. You know we have all the rights we need. You though; kidnapping a minor, harbouring a missing person . . . that's *definitely* unlawful.'

'Nobody kidnapped me!' snapped Alice. 'Where are you taking us?'

The man didn't bother to talk to her. He just slammed the door and they sat in silence for a few seconds in the dim late-evening light that shafted in through letterbox-sized panels of glass in the vehicle walls.

'Sorry, Alice,' sighed Caroline.

'It's not your fault,' Alice said.

'I should never have encouraged you to leave home,' said Caroline. 'You might have been able to convince them you knew nothing . . . you might. Now, though . . .'

'It was *my* decision,' said Alice. 'And I'm glad. I don't regret it.'

'Yet,' muttered Caroline.

34

He rolled over on the ground, inhaling the scent of pine needles and earth. Long slow breaths helped him get over the nausea.

'You all right, mate?' whispered Olu, a dim shadow nearby. Dax shifted to fox and heard Olu gasp. 'Wow—man—that is . . . off the scale cool.' Dax realized it was the first time he had shifted in front of Olu.

In fox form his weakness fled and his senses took charge. A mound rose about fifty metres north of them, clear of any tree cover. No fence surrounded it; they must already be inside the perimeter. A chalky white line gleamed through the grass, scrub, and lichen on the mound—part of the concrete arch that sheltered the blast doors in the side of the hill.

A weed-strewn tarmac road led to the arch and Dax could see that lighting rigs of some kind had been set up at intervals along it. The lights were not on, though. He guessed they would be running on sensors—and spring to life the moment anything larger than a bat crossed the path.

'I can't go any further in,' said Olu. 'The sensors might pick me up if I move any closer. I'll wait here for you, OK? You got the camera?'

Dax shifted back, nodding, and patted his jeans pocket. Olu screwed up his face. 'How come you can carry that with you when you're shifted, man?'

Dax shrugged. 'Anything I wear or carry with me just shifts with me and reappears when I'm back in boy form,' he explained. 'I know . . . it's weird. But that's how it works.' He shifted to falcon, eliciting another gasp from Olu, and flew up through the trees, high above the compound, scanning it for movement. The area was no more than half a kilometre across—an innocuous patch of green inside an unremarkable stretch of woodland. Further along the weedy road he could see a chain of darkened lights which eventually reached some kind of checkpoint gate—dimly lit—containing at least two people. The high concrete wall on either side of it was covered in ivy and brambles and looked like it had been here since the 1950s. Dax guessed the COLA Project liked to keep it looking much the same as it always had from the outside, to deter too much interest from any passing ramblers. He could see thin wires stretched almost invisibly along it, though, from concrete pillar to concrete pillar, around the entire compound. And he could sense the vibrations from them—shock wires. A modest deterrent. The Project must be confident that it had everything thoroughly covered on the inside of the compound. This place was containing Cat. As after all— and at least two of them could bend pylons and hold back avalanches with their combined talent. What other measures they must have in place made Dax shudder.

But maybe it was just as Caroline had said—all they needed to control their charges was love. And the fear that came with it.

He could see eight pale circles in the grass across the hillside. These must be the vents. Swooping lower, he felt the warm air rising from them. Which to go down? He opted for the middle vent; the most central location. He had no idea where it ended—in a locked laundry room or a septic tank as far as he knew. This was possibly an even more dangerous mission than escaping the dome. At least with the dome he had known precisely what he was up against. He'd had a complete plan.

This time he had only half a plan and no Clive to help him test it. He landed next to the circle of thin metal. It was shaped like a shallow conical hat, attached to four rods which sank into the soil—a cap for the vent to keep rain out. Dax pulled at it but it held fast. He pulled again and felt the structure give just a little. Impatiently, he shifted. A dog otter's strong teeth and powerful neck muscles made short work of ripping off the vent cap. He tossed it aside and then shifted back to fox to peer down the dark shaft. It slid away into gloom and he could just make out distant flickers—light travelling up from perhaps thirty metres beneath him, flickering through the turning fans. The scent carried up to him was neutral—old brick and dusty electrics. No humans.

The first fan was about six metres down. There was nothing else to wait for. He was going to have to try his insane, half-baked plan. Or give up and leave Gideon and Luke inside this hill . . . perhaps for ever. Dax took a deep breath, shifted to falcon, and dropped into the warm, dark well.

He dropped fast but quickly eased his speed with some gentle wing-spreading; giving himself precious microseconds to see the fan below. It was a pale, three-bladed thing, turning lazily, made of plastic. Set into a circular mount, the blades were curved and not viciously sharp, but if he tried to fly through at the wrong angle at the wrong second he could end up getting his neck broken.

He landed on the mounting, digging his talons in fast and steadying himself with his outstretched wings pressed to the walls. Now he needed to get the rhythm. He needed to drop through at exactly the right moment. Against an updraft. With no margin for error. He closed his eyes and felt the vibrations of the machinery. How could he ever get this right? It was insane! He needed to stop the fan.

But how? Wedge it with something? What? For a few seconds he considered flying back up, hunting for a rat or a baby rabbit and then dropping the poor creature down ahead of him. Small dead mammals wedged into the machinery might do the trick. It was a grim plan—but it might be the only way.

Then he noticed something. A thin plastic-coated wire looped up over the mounting of the fan and fed in through a channel. Its power source. Glancing down he could glimpse the flex running down the wall towards the fan below—and presumably all the way to the bottom. The electrics. So . . . what if he shorted out the power? It would be the work of seconds to cut through the wire with his beak or talons. But would that short *him* out too?

No, he told himself. *It won't. If you can get through an electromagnetic dome, you can survive a little bit of static.* The words were hollow but he couldn't just give up because of a flimsy plastic barrier. *No.* Dax sank his talons into the wire and sliced it through. The vent shaft lit up in a tiny firework display and his skull was cracked against the concrete as he spasmed and flopped into the fan, senseless.

He awoke, swinging gently on one of the blades. His brain buzzed and stung and he could smell singed feather. But he was OK. More importantly, he hadn't just been chopped in half or strangled. The blades had stopped. All the way down? He felt less of an updraft and the light was no longer winking and moving as it had before. Had he done it?

He shuddered his feathers back into place, took a breath, and dropped down through one of the three gaps in the fan, before again holding his wings out like a paraglider's chute to slow his descent. He landed on the next fan down, finding it turning lazily to a halt; dropped through, descending again and again until suddenly he was out, free, in a corridor, light bathing him from all directions. He flapped wildly to stop his descent and coasted along just below the ceiling. The corridor stretched away in a gentle curve in both directions, its grey walls lit by round glass lamps in metal cages. The floor was some kind of black vinyl which gleamed like wet tar. A calf-height skirting strip ran along the concrete wall. It was dark grey metal, studded with rows of tiny decorative circles, each the size of a pea. Dax wasn't too interested in the decor—he was scanning for clues on whether this plan could work.

Was he far enough in to bring Olu back here? What if the corridor just led to locked doors? He saw a door now. A brushed steel thing with . . . good news . . . a round glass pane at head height. If they all had windows Olu could simply peer through each door and port along into what he saw.

And thinking of what might be seen, Dax suddenly realized he might be seen himself—on camera. There was—of course—a tiny digital eye set high along the corridor wall—several metres away. Had he been spotted yet? The camera was trained at a downward angle; he was flapping awkwardly above its sight line. Should he land and try a door? The handles were like small wheels—the kind of thing you saw in submarines; probably designed to be turned and sealed against flood or invading enemies or . . . nuclear fallout. This is what the place had originally been built for, after all.

He would have to shift back to boy form to try the door. He had to anyway, to use the camera. He would definitely be seen as soon as he did. Unless . . . Dax flew high, just under the ceiling, to the camera. It was on a small metal stalk with a wire feed running into it. Well . . . it had worked OK with the fan. He landed on the stalk that held the small camera and drove his talon through the wire. This time he got only a small static kick-back; not enough to do more than shake his tail feathers. The red light on the back of the device immediately blinked out. Yes! He had disabled the camera.

He landed on the black floor and shifted back to boy form, crouching low. And instantly felt a series of sharp stings across his legs and arms. He gasped involuntarily but did not cry out. Something weird was in his forearm. It was a tiny black spike—like a thick needle. He realized he had been punctured by six or seven of them; several had gone straight through his jeans. Black spikes. What the hell . . . ? What the hell *were* they?! He tried to pull the one in his arm back out but it sent out a sharp spasm of pain and he realized that it must be barbed—like a fish hook. Each wound was now hot with pain—as if he'd been stung by several wasps.

Now he could hear movement and, somewhere distant, a siren sounding. The little pea-sized holes along the skirting were lit up red and pulsing. Now he realized they were not a design detail. He had triggered some kind of trap! The holes had been loaded with tiny darts! They might be poisoned!

In a microsecond he was back in falcon form and flying for the vent. But no no NO! He had not yet taken a picture. He dropped, shifted again and snatched the camera from his jeans pocket. He snapped several shots of the corridor—ignoring the intense stinging of fresh puncture wounds in his legs as he triggered the booby trap a second time. Then he pocketed the camera and shifted again.

He could hear heavy thudding footsteps and shouts. He didn't wait to find out who was coming. He flew up through the vent, flapping hard to rise in the narrow chimney, flittingly awkwardly through the fans as they idled gently in the rising warm air. Up and up and up. It was tremendously hard and not just because he was so constrained that his wings could not manage a full span. He was weighed down with the knowledge of those darts . . . those poison darts.

At last he reached the top and shot up high into the cool night air. He flipped over and flew in an arrow-straight line back to the woods. Seconds later he hit the soft peaty floor next to Olu and shifted back to boy, groaning and peering at his wounds.

'What happened to you?!' Olu was on his knees, flicking a pencil-thin torch beam across Dax's face. Dax grabbed it and redirected it to his left arm.

'There was some kind of pressure trap in the floor! When I landed as a boy, I got shot full of darts! Look!'

'Man! That's nasty!' Olu peered at the arm wound which was now seeping blood, then down at Dax's jeans where a dozen other wounds were staining the blue denim.

'They're barbed—like anglers' hooks,' grunted Dax. 'I can't pull them out.'

'C'mon,' said Olu. 'We need Mia.' He grabbed Dax and squeezed his wrist hard. But nothing happened. 'Whoa!' said Olu. 'Did you pick up some magnetite?!'

'No!' said Dax.

'So why aren't we going anywhere?'

They stared at each other for a few seconds and then Dax shook his head as the answer dawned on him. 'That's what they are! These little darts . . . they're magnetite.'

Olu backed away from him for a moment, shaking his head. 'Wait,' he said. 'We gotta cut those out of you. I'm getting Mia.'

He vanished and was back in less than thirty seconds, and there was Mia, kneeling at Dax's side and peering at the darts in the dim torchlight. She took his hand and the stinging pain subsided instantly. 'Yes. We have to cut them out,' she said. 'Olu . . . ?'

He handed her a scalpel from his pocket.

'Do you always carry that?' murmured Dax, between shaky breaths.

'Yup,' said Olu. 'To cut magnetite out of COLAs.' He didn't laugh as he said it.

Now, as Mia angled the scalpel towards his arm, Dax could see the dart was a deep reflective grey colour; not black. 'So—they've designed that system just for Olu,' said Mia, sounding awed.

'Wow! Just for me!' murmured Olu. 'So . . . what— it's triggered by the sudden arrival of ten stone of sexy cool black guy, busting a hole in the laws of physics?'

Mia was using the blade now. She cut quickly into the

wound and withdrew the small, barbed dart, dampening his pain with instant Mia Effect. 'Pressure sensor in the floor, I expect,' she said. 'Something over a certain weight lands on it without warning and POW. It's clever. And now we know about it.'

As Mia swiftly got the darts out she asked the important question. 'Dax, did you manage to get a picture?'

Dax handed her the camera and she scanned the corridor images quickly before showing them to Olu. 'Brilliant!' she said, removing the last dart. Then she winced as she realized what getting those shots must have cost. 'You took pictures while your legs were full of darts?!'

Dax shrugged. 'I set off an alarm too. They were running for my section of corridor as I got out of there. If Olu ports in—even if he finds Gideon and Luke—how will he get them out again, shot full of magnetite?'

'South Korea,' said Olu.

'You what?' said Dax, rubbing his arm where Mia had just healed his wound. (He never could quite get over the wonder of that.)

'Wait here,' said Olu. 'I'll show you.' He vanished.

Mia finished healing his leg wounds and sat back, cross-legged in the grass. She was wearing black jeans, black trainers, and some kind of army-issue green jacket.

'A weird world you live in these days,' said Dax.

'It always has been weird,' she said. 'It's just a new kind of weird.'

'Where's your grandfather? I hope he was worth leaving us behind for.'

She smiled tightly. 'He's family. I need family. He's at home . . . waiting for us.'

Dax bit down on the many other things he would like to say and in the end just settled for: 'Are you happy?'

Her dimly lit face was thoughtful. 'Sometimes,' she said. 'For a while.'

'And other times?'

'Dax—I don't think anyone can claim to be happy all the time. What you're asking me is whether I made the right decision; leaving you all behind. Well—I know I did. My brain knows it. There was no other logical choice. You know it too. But my heart . . . ? Well . . . my heart goes its own way. Sometimes I'm happy. Sometimes I'm . . . desolate.' Her voice grew thin and high. 'I miss you all so much.'

Neither of them spoke for a while, just listening to the gentle wind stirring the needles of the pines above them.

Then there was a small punch of displaced air and Olu was back—wearing new boots. They were black and laced all the way up to the knees. 'South Korean army-issue,' said Olu, panting slightly. 'Reinforced with steel plates under the leather. No darts are gettin' through these babies!'

'Good,' said Mia. 'But you can't go in there now. The alarm has been triggered. Everyone will be on high alert. In fact . . . listen!'

They could hear voices now and see spots of light across the dark woods. And then . . . a chilling sound. Hounds.

'Time to go!' said Olu.

Mia dropped the magnetite darts into a hole in the trunk of a nearby tree. 'OK,' she said, taking Olu's hand. Dax took the other and they left the country.

35

They were taken to a city. Plymouth, Caroline guessed, judging by the traffic noises and the length of the journey. Here they were driven into an underground garage and transferred into some kind of police holding cell. It was a white box of a room with a table and three chairs, bright lights reflecting in a mirror across one wall. It smelt of disinfectant.

'What are they going to do with us?' Alice whispered.

'Question us,' said Caroline. 'Find out what we know. Where Dax has gone.'

'But we don't know where he's gone,' said Alice. She dug her hands into her jeans pockets and turned her little bottle of nail polish over and over in her fingers, trying to be calm. On arrival at this place they had been searched and patted down by a female operative. They'd found her stashed clothes in the canoe and brought them along. They had, at least, given these back to her so she could get out of the diving gear. They'd handed back the contents of her pockets too. Their search had uncovered no weapons, of course. They'd found Caroline's phone, though, and traced the single incoming call on it back to the payphone near Alice's house. Caroline hadn't ever made a call to Dax on the new phone she'd made him take. That was something.

'So . . . when do they interrogate us?' Alice whispered after several minutes had passed.

Caroline raised an eyebrow and nodded towards the mirrored wall. It was pretty odd, come to think of it, that a cell like this would have a mirror. 'Oh my God,' Alice breathed, suddenly. 'It's two way! They're watching us!'

Caroline smiled at her humourlessly. 'And listening. Hello, folks!' She gave a little wave. 'Look—let's save everyone some time and trouble. We don't know where Dax is. We really don't. Get your psychics in for a quick mental pat down and then we can all go home.'

There was silence for a few moments and then a click as the door opened and a tall, lean man with a narrow face and pale grey eyes came in. He stared from one to the other before he spoke in an equally pale grey voice.

'You've already had the mental pat down, as you call it. We know you met Dax earlier today and that he made arrangements to meet Spook Williams and Mia Cooper. We know that's probably who he is with now. The question is why. We imagine he is planning some kind of terrorist assault on this country.'

'That's ridiculous and you know it,' said Caroline.

'Is it?' said the man. He turned to Alice and said, in a kindly voice, 'My name is Malcolm Forrester and I am the head of the COLA Project. Alice, I know you love your brother and want to protect him. Now, I can probably help to get you out of the trouble you're in—

but first you will have to help *me*. We need to get Dax back to COLA Club and away from Mia Cooper and her cell. He is being radicalized, you must realize this. But it's not too late to save him from life in prison.'

Alice shook her head. 'Dax . . . radicalized? How stupid do you think I am?'

'Well, I suppose I'm likely to find out quite soon,' he said, giving her a sudden, cold smile. 'We all want what's best for Dax. We want him safely back at Fenton Lodge. Help me get him back and I will see to it that your life—and the lives of your mum and your dad—carry on just as before.'

Alice said nothing. She tried not to gulp.

'It's not a bad life, is it?' said Forrester. 'Nice house, nice school, good job for your dad, lots of pretty clothes for you. These things can change, though. It's a very uncertain world, Alice. Redundancies, financial problems, huge tax bills that come out of nowhere . . . houses repossessed . . . arrests for credit card fraud. Quite steep jail sentences. These things can happen to the nicest people.'

Alice felt her heart drop. He was blackmailing her. She was being made to choose. Dax . . . or her mum and dad.

'All you need to do, to keep everyone safe,' said Forrester, pulling a small video camera from his pocket, 'is record a little message to your brother. I'm ready when you are . . .'

36

Another morning. Another high perimeter wall. This one was made of pale yellow brick and enclosed a small country estate in Gloucester. The handsome three storey house stood in beautiful greenery and well-tended grounds. An ornamental lake lay to the east of a sweeping paved driveway. At first glance you might think it was a normal health spa retreat—but three fly-pasts had confirmed to Dax that it was all COLA Project business as usual. The pretty lodge house at the main gates of the estate housed the military personnel. It wasn't obvious from the road but they were easily spotted with falcon eyes—along with the blinking lights of cutting edge surveillance tech behind eighteenth century sash windows.

But there was no electromagnetic dome. Either they had decided the Cat. Cs didn't warrant that level of security, or they'd just not built it yet. On a lower pass of the gatehouse he had spotted some more of that metal skirting with its little puncture holes, no doubt primed with more magnetite darts in case of a visit from Olu. He had to admit it was clever. At least it would be, if Olu didn't now know about it. It must have cost millions to develop and install—and all Olu had done was get the right pair of knee-high boots. Still, they might have set the mechanism in other, higher locations elsewhere. Olu needed to be careful.

Dax couldn't risk another low-level recce. He was lucky not to have been spotted so far. There were a good many pigeons and rooks flying around the area as the sun rose, so he'd been able to lose himself among them. He landed back in the tree where Olu sat, outside the perimeter wall, shielded by the summer foliage. 'This is it,' he said. 'Wires along the walls, security staff in the lodge—more of those fun dart-throwers in the skirting boards. Bound to be in the main house as well. Kennels, too, at the back. Sniffer dogs on site.'

'OK—well, let's skip a tour of the grounds, shall we?' said Olu. 'Can you get in the house?'

'Try and stop me,' said Dax. He could sense Lisa. He had sent several telepathic shout-outs as he circled in the sky above. He hadn't got back words from her—but he had received a belt of pure fury and frustration. She was in there. And she was mad as hell.

'I'm going in again,' he said.

'You got the camera?' asked Olu once again. And again Dax patted his jeans pocket. The gadget was tucked tightly inside.

Olu touched his shoulder just before he shifted. 'I still can't get my head round that. How do you shift to a bird and back and not lose all your clothes and stuff in your pockets? It doesn't make sense.'

'And teleporting around the planet *does*?' asked Dax. 'Look—I think it's a field thing . . . the things I wear and carry are in my field of . . . existence. Mia would call it my aura, probably. Anyway, all of that field gets shifted too, so anything in contact with me goes with me.' He shrugged. 'Don't ask for the science!'

'Can you shift people with you too?' asked Olu. 'Could you turn me into a bird? Like I can port people with me?'

'No,' said Dax. 'It doesn't work like that. I wish it did.'

Olu nodded. 'OK.' He let go of Dax. 'Go on then— but don't hang around in there having a reunion. Find your girlfriend and get a photo and get back!'

'She's not my—' but Dax stopped. Was she? Was Lisa his girlfriend? The word seemed ridiculous. Lisa couldn't be a 'girlfriend'. She was much, much more than that. Whatever happened, even if they never shared another kiss, she was so much more.

He flew again and tried to zone in on Lisa's beacon. She had thrown it up as soon as she'd sensed him in the sky above. But it was flaky—wavering—not nearly as strong as he would expect. It took him to the west wing of the house and there was a slightly open window. Nobody was looking out of it but he felt a fresh pulse of Lisa spiralling up from the sill. He landed.

The room was small and had two beds. In one of them was a girl with long dark hair, asleep with her back to them. In the other sat Lisa, in her pyjamas. She was cross-legged—her bunched fist aloft, ready for him to land. He did, trying hard not to pierce her skin with his talons. She held still and gazed at him.

There were shadows underneath her eyes but her face broke into a wide smile. *Dax!* she sent, staying silent to keep the girl in the next bed from waking. *What took you so long?*

Are you OK? He sent back; telepathy, as ever, much easier while he was in animal form.

No! I've been trying to reach you for DAYS! Dax—they gassed us! They bloody gassed us in the bus on the way here! So we wouldn't see where we were going! The driver put on this mask thing and the windows and doors were sealed and this gas came out and knocked us all out. He didn't even change gear! And then I woke up here.

Dax shivered. *What's it like here?*

It's sheer luxury! Anything you want—you get. There are massages and reflexology and yoga classes and loads of touchy-feely love-in sessions between all the healers and psychics. It's AWFUL.

Dax had to laugh. *Sounds like hell on Earth.*

Lisa did not laugh with him. *It's still a cage, Dax. Nobody asked us if we wanted to be here FOREVER, did they?*

He nodded, gravely. *Have you seen where they took Gideon and Luke?*

Lisa put him onto the wooden bedstead and dropped her face in her hands. *Sylv keeps sending me images of an underground bunker. Why the hell didn't she tell me SOONER? Why didn't we get warning? They've separated us all so they can control us. I think they're doing things to us here when we sleep. There's this kind of pulse they play at nights—like sound waves to take you into deep sleep. I feel like I'm drowning in* them. *I don't dream here. I don't get any spirits wandering in at night either.*

Dax tilted his feathered head. *Isn't that a good thing?*

No! It's not! I don't want anyone but Sylv to mess around with my spirits! They don't ask first, Dax—they just do stuff. Did I mention they GASSED us on the bus?

You want to get out of here? he asked. *I can take you away with me now. I've got Olu on standby.*

OLU? Lisa stared at him. *Olu who took Mia? Are you insane?*

I went to Mia for help.

Lisa blinked. *Mia? Mia . . . is helping you?*

Yes. And we're going to get Gideon and Luke out too. Are you coming?

Lisa closed her eyes and took a deep breath. *No.*

What?!

Not yet, she said, opening her eyes again and fixing him with her unshakeable gaze. *You have to get my dad somewhere safe first. I kicked up a lot when we got here . . . and Forrester told me what they'd do if I caused any trouble. He said he'd take it out on Dad.* She gulped. *And I believe him.*

Dax groaned inside his head. *We all have family . . . they will threaten anyone they have to, to keep us under. Alice is on the run.*

What—your little sister? You're kidding me!

No—she's hiding out in Cornwall with Caroline Fisher.

Lisa looked astonished. And then she shook her head briskly. *Dax—go and rescue my dad. Get him somewhere safe. Then come back for me. I won't go anywhere until you've done that.*

Dax nodded. *Where is he?*

Somewhere in Norway! wailed Lisa, dropping her face into her hands. *I think. I don't even trust my dowsing any more. Not since coming here.*

Can you see him? Can you get the image across to Olu?

Is he telepathic? she asked.

No, said Dax. *He's not.*

Lisa stared at him. *I don't know what to do. I just can't be sure.*

He shifted to boy, crouched on her duvet, and fished the camera out. He took a couple of shots. *For Olu,* he sent. *So he can port in. He needs to have seen your room to port into it. Then you'll need to let him cut out your magnetite.*

AFTER you get Dad! She looked at him stonily. *Go to the house! Ask Marguerite where he's gone!*

OK. I'll do that and I'll come back as soon as I can.

AFTER you've got Dad, she insisted. *I won't risk his life.*

He stared at her for a few seconds. He badly wanted to hold her.

No, she sent back, her telepathic voice soft. *It would be hard to let you go—and Tilly could wake up at any moment. But . . .* she sent him an image in which she was holding him too. Dax shivered, shifted, and flew away.

37

'Where's Lisa?' demanded Mia, the second they got back to the house above the vineyards. It was dark in Argentina now, and she was dressed in a short red silk dress and white boots. She looked tense and when she moved her fingers there were sparks.

'She won't come—not until we rescue her dad. She thinks he's in danger if she doesn't behave.'

Mia shook her head. 'So rescue her dad,' she said, glancing at Olu. 'Then go and get her!'

'Not that easy,' said Dax. 'We don't know where he is.'

'He's not at home,' said Olu. 'We went there. He's away, travelling, on business—but "somewhere in Norway" is a bit broad for my talents.'

'So get Lisa to dowse for him!' yelled Mia. Sparks showered across the polished wood floor, striking the pointed toes of Spook's boots as he lounged on a sofa.

'It's too late in the day now,' said Dax. 'There'll be people around her. It'll have to wait until tonight. And even then . . . it's not easy. She's not in good shape for dowsing. They're doing something to their heads; blunting their COLA talents.'

Mia gave a short scream of frustration and Dax felt the air crackle with heat.

Then she took a long breath and the air cooled.

'No,' she said. 'This isn't meant to happen. Not like this. Olu, Spook—the plan.' She looked at her watch. 'There's still time. We can still do it.'

'What plan?' asked Dax.

Spook was consulting his Rolex. 'He'll be there in twenty minutes—they'll both be in their meeting for an hour, at least. St. Evangeline's will be on board the *Countess* in about half an hour—and we still have the *Duchess* on standby. And all the kit. We won't get a chance like this again.'

'What are you *talking* about?' asked Dax.

Spook smirked at him. 'Really, dingo, you don't need to know. We have a plan to save all your little friends, that's all. Just take a nap and let the grown-ups sort it all out.'

'No,' said Mia, as Dax gritted his teeth. 'He comes with us. He'll be useful. Both of you—get over there and set it up. And be quick. Come back for me and Dax as soon as you're done.'

'What the hell is this plan?' snapped Dax, as soon as Olu and Spook had vanished. 'Who are we going to meet?'

Mia turned to him with a smile; all her recent fiery angst evaporated. 'Dax, we're going to meet the Prime Minister. And your friend Forrester.'

Dax gaped. 'How?'

'Well, when I recently met up with Forrester's lovely secretary and saved her from death by brain tumour, she kindly gave me some information about where Lisa and Gideon were being held. And she also gave me some diary schedules for her boss—Mr Forrester. She may not have noticed that she'd done that. Anyway—I know precisely where Forrester will be in about twenty minutes. In a meeting with Jonathan Wheeler, our esteemed Prime Minister, at a secure office building beside the River Thames.'

Dax felt his heartbeat pick up. 'What are you going to do?'

'Well, to be honest, since you made contact with Spook we *were* thinking of just doing nothing. We can probably get Gideon and Lisa—and perhaps Luke—with your help. And that's what we were making this plan for in the first place. So you could escape and come with us.'

'With you? To live with you and Olu and . . . *Spook*?'

Mia shrugged. 'It's not a matter of forcing you,' she said. 'We just thought we'd remind you there's another option. That you don't *have* to be COLA Project slaves. After what Forrester's been doing over the past few weeks, we thought you might be ready to think about another kind of life.'

Dax said nothing. Was he ready for this? *Was* he? As much as he cared about Mia, as much as he'd missed her, he'd never imagined following her into the new life she'd made for herself.

'Our aim was always to get you and Lisa and Gideon and Luke out. Maybe a few others too—but with a different plan. We *could* still forget that plan and just hope that Olu will be able extract Lisa, Gideon, and Luke. I would be happy with that . . . except, with what we now know about the magnetite darts and the security cameras, I'm uneasy. There could be other traps in that bunker and I can't afford to lose Olu. And if Lisa won't come without her dad being taken first . . . it's getting complicated. So—back to Plan A. If we strike it has to be today—in the next hour. I don't have time to explain why—you'll just have to trust me.'

She took his hand and flooded him with Mia Effect. As he floated on the high she was sending, he wanted to trust her. He really did. But that word . . . *strike*.

'Come with us. Be ready,' she said. 'And trust me.'

38

Once Alice had made the video they were taken to another windowless holding cell with two narrow bunks and a metal toilet next to a tiny basin in one corner. There was a curtain you could pull around it.

Neither of them could sleep much, under their thin grey blankets. Alice lay awake, still appalled at what she'd been made to say the night before. She'd hated it. But what else could she do? Their situation rolled around her head endlessly as she tried to work out what she could have done better. How had they been found so fast? Why hadn't she made a better code to Dax in her letter? Why hadn't she been more careful not to be followed?

'Alice, stop beating yourself up. It was me—not you,' said Caroline, around 6 a.m. 'I made it too easy when I left that note on the roof for Dax. They obviously guessed that the location we'd have in common was Tregarren College. They probably tracked me even before then . . . they might have found out I'd gone to Seth's place and borrowed his bike.'

'Doesn't matter anyway,' said Alice. 'We screwed up.'

'You'll be OK,' said Caroline. 'You've got family on the outside; they won't dare to keep you for long.'

'I think they dare do anything they like,' muttered

Alice. 'Damn!' She suppressed a whimper. 'I just bit a nail off!'

They ate a breakfast of tepid scrambled eggs and toast and then one of the Control people told them they were being transported to the COLA Project HQ in London. They were told to use the toilet and be ready for another long journey in the truck.

'I don't feel well,' said Caroline.

The young woman in a black suit eyed her closely. 'Do I need to get the duty medic in to check you?' she asked, tersely.

'No, I'm fine. Just didn't sleep well,' said Caroline. 'I can do without COLA Project TLC thanks very much. Are you OK though, Alice? Not still hot?'

Alice blinked, not understanding. Then she saw Caroline raise one eyebrow a fraction and realized she needed to play along. 'I'm OK. I was feeling quite hot in the night though. And my head's aching but that's probably just the horrible pillow.' She stared resentfully at the Control woman. 'It's like sleeping on a biscuit. You should try it some time.'

Caroline stood up and stretched, wincing. She briefly massaged around her neck and shoulders. 'I ache,' she said. 'Tell the hotel manager to get better beds in. The en suite's not up to much, either. I won't be posting a five star review.'

The Control woman stared at her humourlessly and then told them to be ready to leave in ten minutes.

Alice flushed the toilet and muttered 'What was that

about?' under cover of its noise. She couldn't see obvious signs of bugging in here but she didn't trust anything about this place.

Caroline turned the taps on and muttered back, 'Probably nothing. Just a thought. Go along with me if I say or do anything else, OK? Even if it sounds barmy.'

Alice nodded.

The truck was the same as yesterday's and once again they were cuffed by one wrist to the bench seat inside it. Yesterday a guard had sat in with them but today they just slammed the rear doors shut leaving Alice and Caroline alone. Their personal belongings had been collected from the holiday home, bagged up and thrown in with the driver. Clearly Control had what they needed, thanks to whichever COLA psychic had been brought in (Alice was guessing *not* Lisa), and were merely going through formalities now.

The vehicle began to move, smoothly at first, as it exited the complex and then more bumpily as it hit the Plymouth roads and began to navigate the early morning traffic. Soon the twisting and turning and occasional bumps told Caroline they were driving along the edge of Dartmoor, heading north. She glanced up at the camera in the corner of their moving cell and slid along the bench towards Alice who was slumped just under it. The camera angle could probably only catch the top of her head from behind. 'How are you feeling?' she asked Alice.

'Had better days,' grunted Alice.

'You look a bit sick to me,' said Caroline, in a voice just loud enough to hear over the engine.

'Do I?'

'Yup.' Caroline's voice dropped again 'Can I have a look at that lovely nail polish of yours?'

Baffled, Alice found the small bottle in her pocket with her free hand.

'Not too obvious,' said Caroline. 'Just let me reassuringly squeeze your hand.' She reached across and gave Alice's hand a squeeze, palming the bottle of polish into her own.

'What—?'

'Shhh,' said Caroline. 'You do look a bit ill, you know.' She winked. In the pocket of her leather biker's jacket she felt the slimy remains of the scrambled egg she'd shoved in at the end of breakfast. Settling back in to the corner opposite Alice, she unscrewed the scarlet polish, casually raising one knee to shield it from the camera.

'Not really the time for a girly makeover,' grunted Alice.

'Nope. Great for a spot of make-believe though,' whispered Caroline. 'Are you ready for an escape attempt? There's a button on a laptop I need to press.'

'You think we can?' Alice mouthed, wide-eyed.

'Nah. It'll probably fail, but hey . . . what have we got to lose?'

39

The driver was tense. He did not like traversing Dartmoor. They should have stuck to the A road but there had been a pile-up just before Bickington and the road was jammed. The tailback might be crawling for hours. They'd had to cut a corner towards Okehampton. It was just him and the special op in the seat next to him. Anything involving the COLAs normally had a cavalcade of armoured vehicles but Control had downgraded the two in the back as low risk. Neither of them had any superpowers, after all. Just a hack and a teenage girl. Not his toughest assignment ever.

But this terrain made him nervous. Driving past a bunch of bikers outside a pub ten minutes back had made his hackles rise. No reason for it. Plenty of bikers were out on jaunts across the summer. Up pretty early, though, weren't they? For a bunch of hairy blokes who'd probably drunk a fair bit last night. But then, bikers liked to catch the roads early too, to enjoy a clear run.

There was a thump on the metal behind them. Then another. He and the special ops guy looked instantly at the screen on the dashboard with its camera feed from the back. One of the females was thrashing about. The other one was dangling from her cuff, sprawled off the bench.

'What the—?' The special ops guy whacked up the volume on the feed.

'—ICK!! Stop the van! She's SICK! We're both SICK!' screamed the woman. She sounded hysterical.

The men glanced at each other and then the driver pulled over to the edge of the road. There was nobody in sight except a lone biker who passed them and sped on.

'Better go and check it out,' sighed the special op. 'Notes said they were feeling rough this morning.' He went around to the back and unlocked the rear doors. What he saw there made him instinctively clap his hand across his mouth and nose. A rumbling sound went through his head. He was not employed for his tendency to panic but the image before him would make even a hardened professional gulp.

The girl lay half on the floor, her eyes fluttering up into her head. Yellow lumps of vomit tracked across her pink T-shirt, but car-sick kids were nothing new. It was the blood trickling from her nose—and her eyes—that abruptly closed his airways.

'GET HELP!' screamed the woman. 'It's bad! It's really BAD! Oh God! I didn't believe him. I didn't think he'd really get involved in it . . .' She coughed into a tissue and then whimpered—staring at a great bloom of red across the white. 'Oh my God . . . we're infected!'

He began to shut the door. 'WAIT!' she screamed. 'At least let me unlock the cuffs. I need to get her into the recovery position! She'll choke to death if she vomits again!'

The special op unhooked the cuffs key and threw it in to her before bashing the door shut. The rumbling in his head was even louder. Biological warfare was the thing that scared him the most.

He ran back to the front. 'Drive!' he said. 'I'm calling this in now. They're bleeding and vomiting. It looks like they've been exposed to something. It could be Ebola or Anthrax or God knows what these rogue COLAs have created . . . We need to set up a quarantine zone. DRIVE!'

The driver turned slowly to look at him. 'How?' he said.

Special Op guy finally looked through the windscreen. The rumbling through his head had not actually been caused by panic but the engines of around thirty motorcycles. The Hell's Angels Cornish chapter filled the B road in front of and behind the truck. Special Op guy cursed loudly and got out, yelling at them to disperse. He hadn't even locked the back door. It couldn't be opened from the inside—but . . .

Shouting at the leather-clad mob, he heard the door open before he even reached the rear of the truck. He screamed 'THEY'VE GOT EBOLA!' to frighten them off but all he heard was gales of laughter and the throttling up of multiple Harleys, Yamahas, and Triumphs.

He didn't even *see* the girl and the woman again. Someone bodyslammed him to the ground and sat on him—a fat guy in leathers that smelled like a damp dog. By the time he'd got up, dazed, the bikers were speeding away in a cloud of red dust. All he found in the back of the van were the empty cuffs, some scrambled egg, and a bottle of red nail varnish, spilling across the floor.

40

'Cleaners. Everyday glamourists. They come in at dawn and dusk like some shadowy, crepuscular animal. Even when they're in full view, people look right through them as they go about their tasks. They're invisible. It's almost a COLA power.' Mia checked the metal shields inside her knee-length white boots—a perfect match for the long white leather coat she'd thrown on over her dress. Behind her, Spook rapped his knuckles on his black velvet jeans. The calf area rang dully. He too had put metal shields around his lower legs and inside his navy suede ankle boots. Dax had no idea where the shields had come from, but Olu had an apparently inexhaustible supply of useful stuff to hand. It seemed he could reach into any props cupboard in any part of the planet as easily as down the back of a sofa.

'So cleaners are a brilliant resource for the likes of me,' Mia went on. 'I make them happy and then they make me happy—by taking photos of their workplace for me. Sometimes they get money; sometimes they get healthier. Nobody challenges them because nobody really sees them. Apart from me. Do you know, a cleaner has never let me down yet?'

Thirty seconds later, the value of cleaner intel was proven.

The prime minister was at a polished mahogany desk; sitting opposite him was the tall, angular Forrester. A high window revealed a panoramic view of the River Thames in the bright morning sun as it flowed past and the giant wheel of the London Eye on the opposite bank. The two men were deep in conversation, with some kind of dossier spread out between them. Mia, Olu, Spook, and Dax arrived almost silently, their feet planting softly on thick oriental carpeting. There was just a push of displaced air and then some tiny patters as the magnetite-loaded skirting strip was activated and barbed darts shot across the room.

The first Forrester knew about it was when a dart hit *him*. He gave a small grunt, glanced down, and saw the tiny post pinning his grey trouser leg to his calf. Then he and the PM spun around to see the trio of teenagers standing by the elaborate Edwardian fireplace. The PM's eyes bulged and he paled instantly as he recognized the girl with the peregrine falcon perched on her shoulder.

Forrester, though, stood up, reached across, and pressed a button on the PM's side of the desk. At once an alarm went off; a siren blaring through the whole building.

'You just made a big mistake,' said Forrester, eyeing them all in turn. 'You're not going anywhere, you know.'

'Well, really,' said Mia. 'We only just got here!'

'What—what do you want?' said the PM, battling to keep the panic out of his voice. He was a pudgy-looking man with thinning brown hair and an oily sheen across his face.

'A trade,' said Mia. There were shouts and heavy footfalls outside. Dax tensed as he waited for the door to be smashed open.

'You're in no position to trade,' said Forrester. 'What are you going to do? Set fire to everyone? And then what? Your young teleporter can't take you anywhere now, can he? Look at yourselves . . . you're riddled with magnetite!'

Olu looked down at the spikes in his boots and grinned. None had pierced through the metal and reached his skin—and magnetite could only stop a teleport when it was in direct contact with the skin.

'Here's what we want,' said Mia, as if Forrester had never spoken. 'We want all the COLAs given back their freedom—and returned either to their families or to Fenton Lodge, if they so choose. We want David Chambers back at the head of the COLA Project and we want regular contact with him and every Child of Limitless Ability and their fathers—at least once a month.'

The door smashed open. Three armed security officers entered, shouting 'GET DOWN! GET ON THE FLOOR!'

And Mia set them on fire.

41

Dax gave a piercing cry of horror and flew up to the ceiling. The shockwave of the fire raced around the room but only the three armed men were hit by it; their weapons instantly turning to molten, dripping metal and their clothes erupting in red, yellow, and blue flame. Their screams were chilling; sickening—even Olu and Spook, backed up against the fireplace, were grimacing.

Mia continued to talk to the PM. 'Our demands are not unreasonable,' she said. 'Consider us the OFSTED inspectors of the COLA Project. If our findings are disappointing we will take action; but if we are happy that you are running things correctly, we'll leave you to continue. I think—' She paused and sighed sharply; the gurgling cries of the burning men were hard to compete with. She stopped the flames with a look and the men fell to the carpet, smouldering. She sent a wave of Effect and their cries turned to soft moans.

Dax shifted to boy, sitting on a high cabinet. 'Mia! For God's sake! Help them!' His voice was high and full of revulsion. He hardly recognized it. The smell of cooking skin was in his nostrils.

'I might help them,' said Mia. 'But that really depends, doesn't it? Do we have a deal, Prime Minister?' She took a thick blue envelope from an inner pocket in her white leather coat, revealing a flash of the red silk dress beneath. 'I have a legal document drawn up—all you have to do is sign it. In triplicate.'

'We do not negotiate with terrorists,' croaked the PM. He looked waxy and his eyes did not meet hers.

'Well, isn't it a good thing we're not terrorists, then?' Mia said. 'We're not seeking to change your way of life or press you into a new religion or to give up some land for us. We don't even want money. We genuinely only want to help you.'

'Mia,' said Forrester. And he did maintain eye contact. 'I realize you're upset about your friends being separated—but I don't think you really understand what's happening here. It's all purely for their own safety. We can't undo everything we have just set up; we have invested millions—*billions* even—in looking after the COLAs. You know how vulnerable they are. They must be protected.'

'They must,' agreed Mia. 'From *you*. Look at you both—you're terrified. And that's the problem. Your fear leads to very bad decisions. David Chambers never feared us and that's why he kept control. He understood. But you don't. And if you get any more scared there won't be a bunker deep enough to store the COLAs, will there? You'll come up with a solution which is much, much more final.'

From his position on the cabinet, Dax saw Forrester reach into his jacket pocket.

'Really, Mr Forrester?' said Mia, raising one eyebrow. 'You want to try some weaponry on me?'

'No, I don't,' he said. He held out his palm and the smartphone resting on it. 'I just wanted to show you all a message.'

He pressed the screen and tilted it so they could see. At once a girl was shown in freeze-frame on the screen. He jabbed the play symbol with his finger and the girl began to speak.

'Dax . . .' Alice looked pale and terrified. 'I'm sorry Dax . . . but they . . . they say if you don't come back, I won't ever see you again.'

Dax felt fresh horror prickle through him. They had Alice!

She was crying now and her hair was clumped and straggly, flopping over her face. She looked young, vulnerable, and crushed. 'And I won't see Mum or Dad or anyone . . . ever again. Dax . . . They've got Caroline too. It's all over.' Her voice was a thin whimper of fear. 'They really mean it.'

He didn't even know what form he took when he attacked Forrester. He was nothing but animal. Only claws and fangs. He was at the man's throat in an instant and Forrester was screaming and trying to fight him off and in the end it was Spook and Olu who pulled him away. Forrester lay on the carpet, clutching his throat, blood seeping between his fingers.

'That's you, is it?' spat Dax, now back as a boy. 'Protector? You threaten little girls to get what you want?!'

Mia stepped over the collapsed, burnt men and closed the door. The sirens were still ringing outside and more movement could be heard in the stairwell. She sent a ball of white hot fire into the metal door handle. 'That should keep your reinforcements out for a while,' she said. 'The lock is melted in an interesting new shape. Now—gentlemen, please can we talk reasonably? The Mexican stand-off thing is just tiresome. I hurt your men; you hurt Dax's sister. Dax bites Forrester—you break Caroline Fisher's legs. I mean—we could go on all day like this. You need to really understand what you're up against. So, please, come to the window. Let's take in the view for a few moments.'

Forrester staggered to his feet, still holding his throat. Dax could taste the man's blood. He wasn't sure how much damage he'd done but he guessed if the man could stand up, he'd probably not actually ripped right through his airway. And he would have, if Spook and Olu hadn't stopped him. Just like his vision on the mountain. The thought made him go cold.

'I'm bleeding,' gurgled Forrester. 'A lot.'

Mia sighed impatiently and touched a hand to his wound. He flinched with fear but the bleeding stopped. 'Now watch,' said Mia.

The building was right on the bank of the river and the river was busy. Pleasure boats and river taxis motored along it. 'See that boat over there?' said Mia. 'Watch it closely.'

There was a moment of silence during which Dax felt a wave of absolute dread.

Mia put her lips close to the PM's ear and whispered: 'This what you get . . . when you mess with us.'

One of the pleasure boats exploded in flame.

42

The PM staggered against the window frame with a gasp of horror. 'Oh dear God,' he moaned.

But Forrester clapped a hand on his shoulder and said: 'It's just an illusion, sir. It's not real. Remember what the red-haired boy can do . . .'

'My name,' came an icy voice, 'is Spook Williams. And yes—I can do that. And a lot worse.' The window shimmered and Dax realized Spook was creating an illusion. He shifted back to falcon and landed on Spook's shoulder to see it. As a part-time animal he had always been resistant to the illusionist's glamour (something that Spook detested in him) but could pick up a pale image of it if he was in contact. Now he saw that Spook had turned the window view into a hellish gaping mouth with a quivering purple tongue and needle-sharp fangs.

The two men instinctively backed away but as soon as they had, the vision was gone. 'That's illusion,' said Spook, shrugging Dax off his shoulder. 'But what's out there is not. She doesn't need my help.'

Forrester threw up the sash and at once the smell of burning flooded in. Dax landed on the fireplace mantel and watched Mia, appalled. Her face was utterly composed. She was burning people alive and she wasn't even twitching. It couldn't be true! This couldn't *be*.

He shot out through the window and down to the river where there were screams from the pleasure boat—and from tourists on the bank and in nearby cruisers. Several little girls in burgundy school uniforms were staring down from the viewing deck of a similar cruiser nearby. Feeling sick, Dax swooped low to the flaming craft. He could see movement through the windows, figures writhing in the smoke, and he could hear awful, shrill, screaming. The smell and the heat were unmistakable. This was no Spook illusion.

At the front of the boat, a man staggered out of the wheelhouse, his back on fire, and leapt into the river. He went under in an instant, the flames doused by the Thames, but he didn't come up. Dax flew into the water and as soon as he was under, shifted to otter. He plunged on down through the brown silty flow, following the flailing hands of the skipper. He reached the man in seconds and sank his teeth into his jacket collar, wrenching the semi-conscious body back up to the surface.

The man's eyes were closed. He made no effort to swim as Dax hauled him along. There was nobody close enough to drag him from the water. Boats were coming but they were being held back by the blazing cruiser as it drifted in a circle, sending a spiral of dense black smoke into the sky.

Then someone threw a ring—a life saver from the

bank. Dax swam hard, dragging the man towards it, keeping his face clear of the water by continually bucking him upwards with his strong otter back and tail. They reached the buoyancy aid and thankfully the man came to enough to instinctively grab it, allowing Dax to duck away underwater and head back to the boat. But it was hopeless. Even under the water he could hear there was no more screaming. It was too late. Mia. His friend. A person he would once have trusted with his life. Mia— had just *slaughtered* a boatful of innocent people.

Caroline Fisher's words came to him: 'If you're bringing big guns back with you, you'd better make sure the safety catches are on.'

Mia had no safety catch.

Seconds later he was shooting back through the window. Outside emergency vehicles were converging on the scene, by road and river. It was pandemonium. But inside the office all was still. Icily still. The burnt men by the door were silent. Dead? No. He could see them breathing and twitching.

Olu had gone but Spook still stood against the fireplace, his face as calm and impassive as Mia's. Forrester and the PM were slumped against the edge of the desk, looking ashen.

Dax landed back on the cabinet and shifted back to boy. 'WHAT HAVE YOU DONE?' he screamed at Mia. 'WHAT THE HELL ARE YOU?!'

She sent him a big wave of Effect but it only enraged him further. 'I don't know you!' he hissed. 'I don't have any idea who you are any more. You've turned into something inhuman!'

'Hush, Dax,' said Mia. 'We'll discuss my humanity later. Are you ready to sign yet, Mr Wheeler?'

The PM did not respond. He was probably in shock, thought Dax.

'No?' said Mia. 'OK—well, one more demonstration. Do you see that other boat? The one trying to motor away from the fire but not getting very far?'

Dax stared through the window. The boat with the schoolgirls on. Did she mean that? A fresh horror took him and he gave a low groan. 'Mia—no!'

'Here, try these,' said Mia. Spook was handing her some compact binoculars which she passed to the PM. He took them with shaking hands, put them to his eyes and trained the lenses on the boat. Some of the children were up on the deck again.

'It's a lovely day for a school trip, isn't it?' said Mia. 'I wonder who those lucky schoolgirls are? Can you read the badges on their blazers? Looks like . . . St. Evan . . . St. Evangel . . . ine's? St. Evangeline's School. Yes, that's it.'

'NO!' shrieked the PM. 'Not Charlotte! NO!'

'Yes! Your daughter is on it,' said Mia. Her voice was cheery. 'Little Charlotte. She and I have already met, don't you know? At a sports day last week. Such a pretty little thing and very good at hockey. She told me all about the boat trip today. She was so excited.'

The PM was chalk-white as he clutched the windowsill. There was a sudden thump on the door and shouts as more security people tried to get through.

'I would say we've got about thirty seconds,' said Mia. The man made no response. 'Still not sure?' She waved at the window and instantly Olu punched back into the room.

He didn't even flinch as the magnetite barbs hit his boots this time. He was occupied with the seven-year-old girl he was carrying. 'Say hello to Daddy,' he said, and the small figure turned and stared, wide-eyed at her father, for two seconds before she and Olu were gone again.

'I'll sign it!' bawled the PM and Mia opened the document on his desk. He signed it and then twice more, on copies, as Olu ported back in alone.

'Thank you,' said Mia, her voice rising above the crashing and splintering on the other side of the door and a helicopter which was now descending outside the window. 'All your instructions are in the copy you're keeping. You've got four hours to comply before we take further action.' She stooped down and ran her fingers across the bodies of the three burnt men and Dax saw their hideously raw, blistered skin slowly pale and smooth and repair itself under the smoking fragments of their clothes.

'That'll do,' she said and took Olu's hand. Spook took the other. 'Are you coming?' Mia asked him. He flew to her shoulder, still shaking with fury.

And then, just before they ported out, Mia torched the second boat.

43

As soon as they hit the polished floor of the vineyard house, Dax was pinning her to the ground. 'YOU WITCH!' he screamed and then his vocal chords were only fit for snarling as he shifted to otter and knocked her jaw up with his powerful snout before pressing fangs against her throat. The burning men, the drowning skipper, and the little girl . . . the terrified little girl. It had snapped something inside him.

He smelt her blood and her Effect and his love for her, as it left him, twisted like a blade in his heart. Spook was on him next, trying to drag him off, but Dax just turned and bit deep into his thigh, making him shriek with pain and stagger away. Then he was back to Mia, pinned to the floor, her violet eyes wide and scared and her breath coming fast, and his mind was racing. He should end her now. How could he let such a monster walk this Earth? Why wasn't she fighting him? Why hadn't she just set him on fire? He trembled with one more moment of indecision and then he found himself underwater. An icy blast of ocean made him loosen his jaws and Mia floated away in bubbles of blue and vanished in the arms of Olu.

He swam in circles. Round and around and around while his head threatened to explode with fear and rage and panic. Eventually he surfaced and saw icebergs. He clawed his way onto the white crystalline shelf of the nearest one and felt the cold seep through his thick fur. Yes, he was an otter, but not built for the Arctic or wherever Olu had dumped him. He must shift and fly. And he would ... he would ... when he just got one spark of energy back.

Dax slumped onto the ice and felt consciousness desert him.

44

He woke up wrapped in blankets in a wicker chair. He was back in the vineyard house and the room was empty. He got shakily to his feet. His clothes were dry. How long had he been here? He heard voices on the deck outside and walked out to find Mia, Spook, and Olu having a meal at the garden table. They all looked at him warily as he stepped towards them. Mia's throat was in one piece but red bite marks still patterned it. She obviously still struggled to mend herself, even with all her superpowers.

'Nice swim?' asked Spook, taking a sip of red wine.

Dax ignored him and looked at Mia. 'I tried to kill you,' he said.

She nodded, touching her throat. She looked a little lost; no longer the villainess. 'I know. I was there.'

'So why am I even here?' he asked, coldly. 'Why am I not frozen to death on an iceberg? Or burnt to a crisp? What's stopping you, Fire Queen?'

'Dax . . . I . . . you don't understand what happened.'

'Oh I think I do. I saw it. I *felt* it. You cooked a boatload of innocent people. And then—for a laugh—you blew up another one, full of kids. CHILDREN, Mia! You killed CHILDREN!'

'No, she didn't,' said Spook. 'Nobody died. It was all a trick.'

'It was NOT,' cried Dax, his voice cracking. 'Remember—I'm resistant to your glamour! I saw what really happened. I had to save the skipper of the boat. He was on fire and he dived into the river and was drowning. I got him out. And I heard the *screaming*!'

'The fire was real,' admitted Mia, her voice soft. 'I did that. And there *was* screaming—but the boat was empty. We set up a soundtrack of screaming in the PA system—and some extra visual effects which I set off remotely.'

'What?' Dax sank to the steps on the edge of the veranda, wondering if he was losing his mind.

'We got into Forrester's diary five days ago,' said Spook. 'We knew he had a two hour meeting scheduled with the PM. And Mia already knew what Jonathan Wheeler's daughter was doing that same day—sailing right past her dad's office that very morning. We were thinking about a straightforward kidnap but it's a bit ordinary. No style. A bit of spectacle always helps, doesn't it? And this was too good a chance to miss. So we hired another cruiser and sent it down the river at just the right time . . . five minutes ahead of the boat with the PM's kid on board, on her school trip. Boat one was the convincer. I could have just thrown an illusion but we knew Forrester would be on to that immediately—he knows about my powers. It had to pass the reality test. As far as the skipper was concerned, he was motoring down to collect our party further along the river as soon as we called. He had no idea Olu and I had been in and set up a bit of theatre.'

Dax shook his head in disbelief. He stared at Mia. 'So the skipper catching fire and nearly drowning was an added bonus?'

She looked away across the valley and tapped her fingers on the table top. 'It was unfortunate. People get hurt sometimes.'

'And the kids on the boat trip?' said Dax, staring at her coldly. 'Was that "unfortunate" too?'

'Dax, for God's sake—that *was* an illusion,' said Mia. 'What do you take me for? You only saw it because you were on my shoulder and I was holding Spook's hand.' She glared at Spook. 'He just couldn't help himself.'

'It was a distraction!' protested Spook. 'To keep them off our trail!'

'We don't HAVE a trail, you ponce!' said Olu. 'Nobody's going to follow ME! You just can't help yourself, can you? All the world's a stage, eh, mate? And because of your massive ego, Mia nearly got her throat ripped out.'

There was a long, uneasy silence. Dax realized, again, that he liked Olu.

And how did he feel about Mia? Numb. Confused. And utterly without trust.

'Did it not occur to any of you to TELL me what the plan was?' he said, glaring around at them all.

'We didn't have time,' said Mia 'And . . . I knew it would work better if you didn't know. Your genuine reactions would make the convincer even more . . . convincing.'

Dax said nothing. He had been used. That was all.

'It's time to go,' said Mia, checking her watch. She had changed again—this time into a black denim jacket and jeans and black zip-up boots. 'The PM will know Spook's ego trip was just an illusion by now. His daughter is safe, as promised. If he's kept his end of the bargain, we'll know in the next twenty minutes.'

Olu got up and held his right hand out to Mia and his left towards Dax.

'Ahem,' coughed Spook, standing up and swinging his leather coat onto his shoulders.

'You're not coming,' said Olu.

Spook looked furious. 'Mia—tell him.'

'I already did,' said Mia, taking Olu's hand. 'You can't be trusted not to show off, Spook. You're staying here.'

Spook slammed his hands onto the table. 'Now look—I am as much part of this as the rest of you,' he snarled. 'Don't you dare leave me out. I want to see this through—I want to watch them cave in to us!'

'C'mon,' said Olu, holding his other hand out to Dax.

But Dax didn't take it. 'Wait,' he said. 'Come and talk to me.' And he walked back into the house.

In the reflection of the glass patio door he saw Olu consult with Mia, shrug, and then follow him in, leaving her to Spook's angry shouting.

'What's up?' he asked when they were both inside.

Dax turned to look at him levelly. 'I'm not one of

Mia's merry men. I'm not going to follow her about, doing her bidding.'

'Mate—I don't think she has you down as that guy,' said Olu. 'I mean—you really do your own thing like nobody I ever met.'

'Yeah? Well, I've still been played, haven't I?' said Dax.

Olu shrugged again. 'So—what do you want? We're going to get your friends back. Don't you want to be there?'

'Yes—but on my own terms. Can you take me somewhere near? Just me? Show me where it is from a distance, where we won't be seen—and then port me again to about five kilometres away? It'll be better that way, trust me.'

Olu nodded. He glanced back at Mia who was coolly regarding Spook as he ranted on. 'You need her permission?' asked Dax, arching an eyebrow at the teleporter.

He gave a tight smile and shook his head. 'I don't need anyone's permission, mate.' And he put out his hand. Dax took it and crossed the planet once more.

45

'I followed you,' said Seth. They were in full public view in the back garden of a country pub, but Caroline had never felt safer. Thirty-six of the Cornish chapter's most committed Hell's Angels were camped around them, enjoying breakfast.

'When? Yesterday?' She blinked. 'After a three day wait?! How?'

'Yeah, I took my time.' He grinned at them both.

'How did you know where to go?' asked Alice, pausing in her demolition of a plate of buttered scones.

'She's not the only one with spy tendencies you know,' he said, winking at Caroline. 'I learned a lot from you, Caro. All my bikes are fitted with the latest tech. There's a tracker in every one, in case it gets nicked. I waited for you to come back and when you didn't, well, I followed you down to the estuary. Just to see what you were up to and, you know, whether we might hook up again. I arrived just in time to see these black Jeeps heading for your hiding place. I hid behind a shed. I saw them take you.' He stared down into his coffee for a few seconds. 'Freaked me out, let me tell you. So . . . I tailed them big black cars all the way to Plymouth nick and watched them go in.'

'But we were there all night,' said Caroline. 'Don't tell me you waited there the whole time.'

'Called the boys in,' said Seth, nodding around him. 'We did shifts, watching the garage exit and all the doors. When your van came out again, I followed again.'

'But how did you know we were still in it?' asked Caroline.

Seth held up his bike ignition key. 'I put trackers in these too,' he said. 'And those coppers helpfully took all your stuff along for the ride—with my tracker in the Triumph key.'

'That is *so* cool,' said Alice.

'So—we picked up some reinforcements along the way,' went on Seth, clearly enjoying himself hugely. 'Got someone to create an awkward little fender bender on the A road, so they'd have to divert and go over the moor . . . and the rest of us thought we might . . . you know—head 'em off at the pass.'

'You cowboy!' laughed Caroline, shaking her head.

'And then *we* stopped the van anyway,' said Alice, gleefully. 'We tricked them!' She was still exhilarated from riding pillion on the back of a Harley Davidson as they'd escaped across Dartmoor. It was the most exciting journey of her life.

'I thought our best hope might be to fake the deadly illness thing, get uncuffed, and then get away across the moor,' said Caroline. 'It was a long shot. I had no idea the charge of the biker boys was right behind me!'

'Here's your tech.' One of the younger, skinnier bikers put a small laptop down on the table with care, opened it, and booted it up. 'Pub Wi-Fi signal is good,' he said.

'Thanks.' Caroline logged on, found the file and the connections she was looking for and took a deep breath, glancing at Alice.

'What will happen?' Alice asked. 'When you hit *send*?'

'A chain of trusted people will get codes,' she said. 'And they have paper instructions safely in their possession to go with the codes. If they don't hear from me again in twenty-four hours they will use the codes, undo the encryption and upload my dossier onto social media, as well as sending it to all the planet's news agencies.'

'Wow,' said Alice. 'You'll tell the whole world about the COLA Project?'

'Yup,' said Caroline, looking slightly pale. 'If it comes to it. But I hope it won't.'

'We should call Dax,' said Alice. 'We have to warn him.'

They went into the pub to use the phone but even as they approached the bar, one of the bar staff was holding the receiver of the landline up and calling out: 'Is anyone here called Caroline Fisher?'

Caroline took a deep breath. They'd been traced again. That was fast. 'Who is it?' she asked quietly. The young woman shrugged. 'Someone called David Chambers.'

46

A cool breeze was buffeting the tussocks of coarse grass, heather, and low-lying trees. They had chosen Exmoor. A central location, miles from any main roads—a high escarpment which gave them a clear 360 degree view in all directions.

The helicopters were already on the horizon as Mia and Olu ported in; three of them, hanging in the sky like black wasps, growing larger with every second. They would be carrying Gideon, Luke, and Lisa—and Alice and Robert Jones. Caroline Fisher, too, if the PM had followed his instructions to the letter.

And Chambers would be there. Chambers would manage the handover; confirm the plan—the way forward. Mia shivered when she remembered her last encounter with Chambers and how close he had come to capturing her and locking her down for ever.

But she didn't hold it against him. She knew he was a decent man, trying to do an almost impossible job—up until he was fired and Forrester brought in. But now he could have his almost impossible job back. Forrester would be sacked and barred from any further involvement with the COLA Project. Life could return to something like normal again. As far as she was concerned, if Chambers simply kept her friends in COLA Club safe and happy without crushing all their hopes of freedom, that was enough. She did not want more right now. Well . . . she did. She wanted her friends back. And she wanted Dax to . . . to what? Mia felt tears well in her eyes and angrily sniffed them away. She did not *do* tears these days. She was strong. But the truth sang through her head regardless: a phenomenal superpower could get you a lot—but it couldn't win you back love and respect. Hadn't she just lost that from Dax?

The choppers landed some distance away and figures descended. They collected together, moving away from the downdraft of the rotors, and one man struck out towards Mia and Olu. Even from a distance she could recognize the steady, economical stride of David Chambers.

Her heartbeat picked up pace. It was nearly done. She had nearly freed her friends and soon they could decide for themselves how they felt about her—and where she took them. They *would* want to go with her. Even if Dax told them everything . . . they *had* to understand she'd done it for *them*.

Half a kilometre to the north-east, Dax watched the choppers arrive and land. He saw the people spill from them and group together on the moor and he saw Mia and Olu, a three minute walk away, waiting.

He also saw a black dot on the horizon. It buzzed like a hornet through the delicate navigational cortex in his brain. Dax felt a sudden surge of adrenalin. What was this? It was moving too fast and too straight to be a helicopter.

He soared across the sky, suddenly understanding. It was a fighter jet. It was heading for the group on the ground and Dax had no doubt what was to follow. It would take out Mia and Olu and anyone else nearby. It might even have been tasked to wipe out all witnesses.

Dax soared on as the jet grew closer . . . and began to realize it was small. Very small. It was a stealth craft, flying low and making very little noise; he could see missiles beneath its wings, primed. He could also see no pilot at all. This was an armed drone. In all likelihood the party on the ground would never see or hear it coming; the noise of the three helicopters would mask it until it was too late. He flew faster than he ever had before, angled down, wings folded in the classic peregrine W. What he was planning to do was ludicrous but he had no choice. It might mean the end of him—but it might mean the saving of everyone he loved.

Back at base, the man who was remotely flying the drone may have been expecting a fireball from the ground. Or some kind of weird illusion which he'd been warned to fly straight through.

What he was not expecting was a fully grown otter at one hundred metres. The impact threw the drone into a spin. On the playback later, the control room would be able to make out a blur of fur and teeth and claws shortly before the camera cut out.

From the ground, nobody noticed the drone dive

beyond a distant ridge. And even when a thin spiral of smoke went up, they were far too engrossed in their own drama to pay it any heed.

'Hello, Mia,' said Chambers. He stood a few strides away from her, hands deep in the pockets of his charcoal-grey trench coat.

'Hello, Mr Chambers,' she said. 'I'm glad to see you back at work.'

'Where is Dax Jones?' he asked.

'I'm not sure,' she said. 'I'm not his keeper.'

'But he *is* involved in this,' pointed out Chambers.

'He helped us, yes,' she admitted.

'Not entirely willingly from what I've heard.' Chambers tilted his head and narrowed his eyes behind his rimless spectacles.

Mia took a breath. 'Let's just say that we didn't always agree on tactics,' she said.

'So . . . you were happy to fry small children, and he wasn't?'

Mia lifted her chin. 'You will know by now that no children were hurt,' she said.

'Are you sure about that?' he asked.

She said nothing. Was she? If any children had been hurt, it wasn't her doing. The PM's daughter might be a bit shocked but she'd get over it.

'I want to talk to Dax,' said Chambers. He sat down, cross-legged, on the grass.

'He's not here,' said Mia. 'Talk to me. I am the one you talk to.'

'Nope,' said Chambers. 'You're not. I mean . . . you are the one who could torch me where I sit, yes—but you're not the one I will negotiate with. I will talk to Dax. Or nobody.'

Mia heard her voice get shrill as she snapped: 'But he's not HERE!'

A dark missile plummeted past her and landed on the grass beside Chambers. Dax shifted to boy, wiping his fringe out of his eyes and panting. There were scorch-marks on his jaw. 'Yes, I am,' he said.

'What happened to *you*, man?' asked Olu.

'Nothing,' said Dax. 'I just had to bring down a bird.'

'Chambers says he won't talk to anyone but you,' snapped Mia. She thrust a folded document at Dax. 'Here is the agreement, signed by the prime minister.' And she turned and stalked away.

'I've read it already,' said Chambers, when they were no longer in anyone else's earshot. He smiled at Dax. 'It's good to see you. What really happened to your face?'

'Our loving government sent a drone,' said Dax. 'Armed with missiles. I took it down.'

Chambers closed his eyes for a few seconds. 'I wish I could say I was surprised. Dax—we meet on new terms. The PM has sacked Forrester—I am back in charge. I must build a truce with Mia and her crew, but I don't trust them any more than I trust Forrester. So . . . are *you* with her now?'

Dax stared after Mia. She stood some way off with Olu, the Exmoor wind blowing at her black jacket and whipping her hair around her face. For a moment he saw the girl he'd first met; gentle, kind, vulnerable. A girl who had saved his life. A lump rose in his throat. Then he remembered her face as she'd set light to the men in the PM's office; coldly amused. He looked back at Chambers and shook his head firmly. 'Never. But I'm not with COLA Club any more either. I won't be coming back. And I don't think Gideon, Luke, or Lisa will, either.'

'Well,' said Chambers, 'in your position I would feel the same. So—once a month—we will communicate. Maybe things will get better and you'll change your mind . . . but for now, let's go with what's set down in this agreement. But with one small amendment—you will be my intermediary. I won't communicate directly with Mia.'

Dax nodded. 'OK—but how will it work?'

'I'll set something up,' said Chambers. 'And I know you won't let me down. Making this truce work will be vital—to be sure the government doesn't crush the very thing it cherishes. I want to keep COLA Club going, Dax—for everyone who wants to be there. And many of them *will* want to stay; they're not all the adventurers that you and your friends are. They need security. Here is my number.' He handed Dax a printed card. 'One week from now, call me. We'll take it from there.'

'You're still working with the government that just tried to drone strike us?' said Dax. 'Really?'

'I never saw the drone and I'd prefer not to know

about it,' said Chambers. 'As it's just failed they will most certainly be needing my services, won't they?' He ran his hand tiredly over his chin. 'What else can we do, Dax? What else can we do?'

Chambers stood up and waved at the group behind him. A knot of them surged forward and in seconds Dax was hugging Gideon and Luke and Alice—even his father. Another fierce hug from Caroline, looking tired but jubilant. And then, at last, holding Lisa close, pressing her head to his chest and breathing into her hair. He could feel her heart beating against him.

'Where are we going?' asked Lisa, pulling away from him to stare up into his eyes.

'Where do you want to go?' came a cool voice. Lisa spun around to see Mia. Mia—a few steps away. Lisa ran and wrapped her arms around her friend, tears spilling down her cheeks. As they held each other close, Dax could see colour spreading miraculously through Lisa's pale skin. It made him ache with some kind of jealousy and anger. Mia just cheated. That was all.

'Dax . . . can we go home?' asked Alice, holding Dad's hand. She looked worn out and Dad looked haunted. 'I miss Mum.'

Dax glanced at Chambers. 'Are they safe? Can they go?'

Chambers nodded. 'You have my word. And you will be checking, won't you?'

'Yes,' said Dax. 'I will. You can go back home on the helicopter, Alice . . . Dad. I'll fly in to see you both in the next few days. Everything will be OK.' He allowed his Dad to hug him, awkwardly as ever.

'And *my* dad?' asked Lisa, glancing at Chambers.

'Turn out he's in Norway,' said Chambers. 'We'll bring him up to speed with everything. He's travelling back now. Do you want to go home to meet him?'

She shook her head. 'Not right now.'

'Our dad too,' said Gideon. 'You have to make sure he's OK! It was bad enough being told he was at death's door when he wasn't. Does he even know what's been happening?'

Chambers shook his head. 'I don't think so. You'll have to forgive me; I still have to get back up to speed. So ... what about you two? If COLA Club is safe again ... will you come back to Fenton Lodge with me?'

Luke and Gideon stared at each other—then went into frantic hand signals, communicating in the way that had become most natural in the past two years. After nearly two minutes of this, Gideon abruptly hung his head and sighed and then looked back at Chambers. 'He wants to go back. He wants to read and study and get a degree in history. He doesn't want to live his life like some kind of superhero.' He gulped back his emotions. 'Can you make that happen for him?'

'Yes,' said Chambers. 'I can. But what about you?'

Gideon gave his brother a tight hug and blinked away tears. His voice was choked when he said 'I'm going wherever Dax goes.'

'So am I,' said Lisa.

'You can all come,' said Mia, her eyes sparkling violet. 'You can all come with me. Olu and I . . . we can show you the world.'

'No,' said Dax. 'I don't want your world.'

Mia closed her eyes. 'You don't know what you're saying . . . what you're turning down.' She opened them again and appealed to Lisa. 'Lisa—I'm your best friend. Trust me. I can give you a life of freedom! Joy! Fun!'

Lisa curled her arm tighter around Dax's. 'I can see in his head, you know,' she said. 'I see all the things you did.'

'But it was for YOU!' cried Mia, tears streaming down her cheeks.

'I know,' said Lisa, wiping away her own tears. 'And thank you. But you've changed and it won't work. I love you. I will always love you. And maybe we *will* meet up sometime; maybe there will be more Lisa and Mia time in this life—but not now.'

'I have *saved his life*!' sobbed Mia.

'And he's saved yours,' said Lisa. 'About ten minutes ago, actually.' She leant in closer to Dax. 'Way to go, Top Gun.'

Dax put his hand out to Olu. 'Somewhere to get some new clothes first—clothes without tracker chips. And then . . . the South of France, please,' he said. 'Me, Gideon, Lisa . . . and . . . Caroline?'

The journalist beamed and skipped across the heather to join the group. 'Oh yes!'

'Olu! Wait!' cried Mia.

'You're not the boss of me,' said Olu, and took them all away.

47

When Olu had gone they all wandered along a river, Gideon and Lisa in new clothes and shoes, and found a pretty pavement cafe. Caroline bought everyone drinks and crepes with the euros Olu had got for them (Dax didn't ask how) and they ate and drank quietly in the afternoon sun.

'We've only got about eighty more euros,' said Caroline, tucking the notes into her jacket pocket. 'And I'm guessing you won't want me to use my cards.'

Dax nodded. 'Guessed right.'

'So . . . where are we going?' she asked. 'How will we live? Olu is gone—he won't be popping in and out to act as an intercontinental taxi service. None of us have our passports and even if we did . . . what's the plan, Dax?'

'We go south,' said Dax. 'It'll take us a few days—walking and bussing maybe.'

'South to where?' asked Lisa. She slid her fingers through his, interlocking them in a way which made a thrill run through him. She had never made a public gesture like this before. He smiled down into her sea-blue eyes, stroked a strand of fair hair off her cheek and said 'Have a look.'

She slipped into his mind as easily as she'd taken his

hand and saw the wide vista of mountains sinking to the sea. 'Spain? We're going to Spain?'

'*Olé*!' grinned Gideon. 'I love paella!'

'You're showing me a cave! Will we really live in a cave?' Lisa was grinning now, excited and happy for the first time in more than a year.

Dax nodded. 'So far off-grid we'll never be tracked down. But just close enough to civilization for me to fly to a phone box and call Chambers—and Mia—every so often.'

'Erm . . . caves?' queried Caroline.

'Yup,' said Dax. 'Cave houses—whole networks of them. People still live in them, you know—really cool people. Cave houses are quite comfortable—and no government tech can get through that much rock. Not even COLA dowsing power can find us there if we don't want to be found.'

'I've always fancied being a caveman,' said Gideon, dreamily spooning up the chocolate sauce from his crepe.

Lisa shivered. 'So . . . we make our own decisions from now on? Nobody . . . protecting us?'

'*We* will protect us,' said Dax.

A smile spread across Lisa's face. 'Nobody controlling us?'

'Nobody,' grinned Dax. 'From now on, we make our own decisions. Don't you think it's time?'

'Nobody feeding us,' pointed out Caroline.

'How do you feel about skinning rabbits?' queried Dax.

Caroline ordered more crepes.

ACKNOWLEDGEMENTS

Many thanks to Dr. Simon Boxall, Southampton University's earth science genius, for guidance on magnetic fields, trajectory, velocity, and other useful stuff. (I've bent science only *slightly*, honest!) Also to Adam Sparkes for useful vent and ducting information (and a slightly sick fan-jamming option!).

ALI SPARKES

Ali Sparkes was a journalist and BBC broadcaster until she chucked in the safe job to go dangerously freelance and try her hand at writing comedy scripts. Her first venture was as a comedy columnist on *Woman's Hour* and later on *Home Truths*. Not long after, she discovered her real love was writing children's fiction.

Ali grew up adoring adventure stories about kids who mess about in the woods and still likes to mess about in the woods herself whenever possible. She lives with her husband and two sons in Southampton, England.

HAVE YOU READ THEM ALL?

THE SHAPESHIFTER